In the Mood for a Melody

Piano Stories

Edited by Joshua Britton

Bird Brain Publishing

Evansville, Indiana

In the Mood for a Melody: Piano Stories

Edited by Joshua Britton

Copyright © 2025

ISBN 978-1-937668-12-9

Cover Layout and Design: Laila Schu - Regent Promotions

Front cover art: Henri Matisse. The Music Lesson, 1916, Oil on canvas. The Barnes Foundation, BF717 (Public Domain).

Published by Bird Brain Publishing

Evansville, Indiana

Bird Brain Publishing is an imprint of Bird Brain Productions.

 www.birdbrainproductions.com

Summary: Seven authors write seven short stories about pianists or pianos.

Paperback printed in the United States of America

CONTENTS

PIANO DREAM

JESSICA HARMAN

MY FATHER AND I sit in a dingy little gyro place in Long Beach, New York.

The rest of the street is teeming with bars. Nightlife: it's Friday night. People are drinking cocktails, getting into a state that they think will lead them to meet someone.

I had a special someone. After fifteen years together, he died. It's one of those things where one regrets not being nicer. He was an artist—a painter—not a musician, like my Dad. But one day, he woke up, and he could sing.

My father told me, when I was a kid, maybe eight, that he dreamed in black and white. This surprised me, because I dream in color.

Getting through life may not be easy, but it's possible. Dreams help. It helps to have something to look forward to, like being a famous musician. Seek your dream.

My Dad taught me how to improvise on the piano to a boogie-woogie blues construct. He sat on the piano bench, and I sat next to him. He taught me how to do what just feels right. And if you do something wrong, make it right with the next note. Harmony, cacophony, rhythm; believe in your song.

As an adult, I have stopped dreaming I can fly. Up over the rooftops, away from my pursuer, or just for fun. Now, at fifty, I no longer dream of flying. No. My dreams are also no longer intricate stories. They're just swampy.

I asked my Dad what he dreamed about while dreaming in black and white. He said he dreamed of a piano keyboard. A piano keyboard is made up of black and white, so he didn't miss much, dreaming in black and white. Sometimes life works that way: it's merciful. Sometimes you don't know what you're missing. Dreams are supposed to compensate us. I wonder if he dreamed of music. I did, once, and it was awesome.

I want to write a story about a piano. It's for an anthology about pianists. So, here is my piano story.

My knowledge of improvising on the piano has served me well. Once, I was in a mental institution. There was a piano. There was another patient in the room, and a staff member. I sat down at the piano and began to play. Out came a masterpiece, as if in a dream where everything is right, and so much better than the reality of the waking world. Was my song in black and white or in color? Or something in a realm beyond color, that speaks of the silvery land of water, water flowing, dreams of music?

My Dad and I sit at our table, waiting for our gyros to be ready, in the restaurant that is predominantly orange with off-white linoleum.

The guy behind the counter comes to our table, bringing our food. It's an extra gesture of kindness that does not go unnoticed by me. My father, too, notices. We say thank-you and smile. We peel back the tinfoil from our gyros, and dig in.

PIANO MAN BLUES

JONATHAN S BAKER

JOEL RUMBLE has accomplished what not one other musician has. He has a captive audience with Rob Austein, the big kicker of the east coast's recording industry. Unfortunately, Joel is the captive. Austein has worked with greats. Name some classic hit that plays in the background in some mob flick, and Austein is the reason that song even got recorded. Austein is also in pretty tight with the men those flicks are about. So, Austein isn't just a power in the music business but in the organized crime business as well.

In between trips to backroom poker games, casinos, and off-track betting parlors, Joel Rumble plays piano, and he plays it well. Mostly radio jingles is what keeps kibble on the table, but he picks up the occasional gig with various artists needing someone to pound the keys. He's on speed dial for about every bar and lounge in town as a substitute. Life for a guy like Joel should be pretty okay. He's talented, has lots of fancy friends. He gets invited to a lot of parties. Thing is, Joel likes the rush of a wager and he can't make a good bet to save his life. Every dime he earns for the next ten years is already earmarked for some bookie or some shark. The kid is skin and bones wrapped in a cheap suit out of a church donation box.

Austein, he ain't lookin' so hot either. The guy is in bed twenty-four-seven three-six-five. He has more tubes coming out of him than a set of bagpipes. He's all yellow right up to his eyeballs. This guy is dying unless Joel wants to keep living.

See, Joel has made another bad bet for the great Don of Recording. Joel, the piano man with no medical expertise what-so-ever, is going to get Austein a liver-hold-the-onions.

Last month, when Joel was taking his bi-weekly beating from Ringo, the bookie Chet "Chedder" Federer's man, Ringo had started to get tired with all the punching and the kicking. He decided to pull a knife to change the pace. That's when Joel got a little scared that maybe this was his last beating, and he started stuttering and muttering crazy ideas.

Joel had heard Austein was sick, like dying sick. He knew the bookie worked for Austein, and so too then did Ringo.

"Ringo, I can help Austein. He's sick, right? I can help you to help him."

"Uhh, you ain't no doc, doc."

"Yeah, but I play over at the Nova Lounge, the country club. I got all kinds of doctor friends. I've heard things about Austein. He's dying. Everybody up the coast is talking about it."

"I don't know about Austein. I know that your name is in Cheddar's book. That's all I know."

"Look just tell your boss. Better yet, don't tell your boss. Go straight to Austein. Then you're the hero. Just tell him Joel Rumble knows doctors."

That is how Joel has ended up here in Austein's private medical suite playing piano for a dying man surrounded by Austein's personal medical staff, while outside, Joel's merry men were hopefully getting a liver without stepping all over it.

After Ringo had gone to Austein's intermediary— a guy named Ludlow—and gave him the rundown, Ringo was ushered through about ten more guys before he got to talk to Austein. Then Joel was dragged one after the other before all the King's men until finally he stood before the man himself. Well, he stood beside him, at bedside. The doctors gave Austein six months without a liver. Austein asked Joel to play him a song. In the next room was a Steinway Model A. Joel played three songs: "Green Onions," "My Funny Valentine," and "The Theme from Cheers." Then Joel gave a vague pitch on the subject of procuring a liver. Austein gave Joel three months to find a liver. At this point it was just one more guy doing the impossible anyway. At the end of that time Joel would have a meeting with Ringo's knife.

Joel does know doctors. Unfortunately they are a bunch of degenerate gamblers and dope fiends, most of whom have lost their right to practice medicine. Now, his brother Jamie Rumble: he is a good doctor with a clean record. He runs a family practice outside the city. A beautiful office where beautiful families come when they have the sniffles.

Luckily for Joel, Jamie loves his wife and kids, but Jamie also can't keep it in his pants. He is always rubbing his sexual exploits in Joel's face. He has to brag to someone and little brother is the only person he knows who wouldn't blab. Joel would never blab, unless it would save his own skin.

So after a somewhat heated bull session over beers with the brother, Jamie, he was in. Every patient coming through his office would be unknowingly tested for match suitability. Data bases would be accessed to find matches elsewhere. Everything was tuning up on the liver search.

Finding a suitable donor was only one wildly difficult and improbable task Joel had to delegate. Separating the liver from the host organism was another task all together, transportation for the item would have to be considered as well. Once the package reached Austein's suite, his team would obviously be able to do what needed to be done.

Joel reached out to Blockhead. Blockhead was a courier, a driver, an escort, a bodyguard, an all-in-one huge angular man who dressed like a pile of dirty clothes. Joel didn't have anything to hold over Blockhead. He didn't need anything. He would work for whoever paid cash and respect. He had carried packages for Austein, collected for Cheddar, and filled in for Ringo. Everybody who depended on Blockhead was satisfied with Blockhead. It's what he lived for night and day. He only needed to know three things; pick up, drop off, and deadline. He named his own price payable on delivery.

With a plan in play, Joel just had to pass the nights without losing his mind. That anxious feeling when a due date approaches with unstoppable force. When he slept, he had visions of Ringo's Blade cutting a sizeable cavity into his own abdomen and reaching in bare fisted to unceremoniously remove Joel's giblets.

Joel had to keep busy. He took every gig he could get. Playing piano anywhere that would have him. He paused between every song to check his phone for the word from Jamie. Finally, one night at the Boca Lounge, a short rat-faced man dressed in a suit like an Oingo Boingo song put his hairy-knuckled hand on Joel's shoulder. It was Chet "Cheddar" Federer, the bookie. Aside from the suit, he still looked bad. He was gleaming with a thick, oily sweat. His eyes were bloodshot. All of this was tinged with the look of anger and great annoyance Cheddar wore.

"What's this about Rob Austein buying your debt? Making me sell it to him at a loss to me. I don't like it. I'm going to take the difference out of you."

Joel looked up at Cheddar with half open eyes. His finger's never stopping. He just shifted effortlessly from "Endless Love" down into "St. James Infirmary." A beautiful African-American woman at the bar had been sending Joel drinks and laughing smiles all night. Joel was currently in a state of bliss, but seeing Cheddar made him reconsider. The sequence of emotions for Joel was bliss, curiosity, a split second of fear, apathy and a return to bliss.

"You'll have to take that up with Austein. He owns me until the end of the month," Joel said.

"After Austein is done. You're dealing with me. No more of that idiot Ringo. I'll cut you myself. I want my pound of flesh, Rumble."

At that moment Joel's phone vibrated on the deck of the piano. Without missing a beat, Joel picked up the phone. He read a message from his brother, the good doctor.

"Hey, you know what, Cheddar? I'll settle up with you at the end of the month. That sounds great. I'll see you then."

Joel stopped playing. He walked away from the piano, away from Cheddar, and over to the woman at the bar. He whispered something in her ear. Together the two left for the door.

Her name was Cleo. She was Blockhead's younger sister. Blockhead had asked her to keep an eye on Joel because he was a reckless man with wild plans and he owed Blockhead money that he didn't have yet.

The drinks she was sending Joel were Shirley Temples and the smiles she was giving him were mostly just because of his acting. When Joel played a gig he would get sloshed or give the appearance of getting sloshed. Tips for the charming, overly emotional, flirtatious, and sometimes surly piano man went up with the perceived level of difficulty.

The message Joel had received was from his brother. He had found the needle in a haystack. The new standard office procedure of running "standard lab work" on every patient had actually worked. It was a man from the city who had come in with what was just a cold. Some random guy comes in demanding to see a doctor. He never saw a doctor but Jamie's well-trained staff took blood for tests and sent him on his way with prescription samples. Guy was pushy as hell, a jerk, and that makes it easier.

The end of the month comes. Joel arrives at Austein's building and is ushered through the lobby and into the elevator leading to an area that had been a recording studio months ago. It was now an operating room filled with Austein's personal medical team, one lone out of place veterinarian with a secret, Ringo, and a Steinway model A.

Dr. Manny Machado was a veterinarian that specialized in horses. Joel had met him at the tracks. Joel got into an argument with Machado after he had euthanized a sure thing that Joel had lost his rent betting on. Joel had told Manny if he had put down the horse before the race, instead of after, then he would have saved Joel quite a bit of money.

Turns out Manny wasn't a bad guy, though. He ended up throwing a couple hot tips Joel's way, and Joel hooked Manny up with a discrete male masseuse with deep probing fingers that could really take the stress away. Joel had a lot of friends. When Joel stood in the Dr. Machado's stables, he was wafting away the smell of horseshit with a fan of glossy portraits of two men in embrace. Manny blushed and was more than happy to help with the liver procedure.

Inside the studio/operating room, Austein orders Joel to play while they wait for Dr. Jamie Rumble and Blockhead to arrive with the package. Joel plays "Sweet Georgia Brown," "Sinner Man," and "The Theme to the Greatest American Hero." The dying old man managed to tap his fingers in time along the bedrail.

Dr. Jamie Rumble arrives stag. For a moment things seem tense. Austein gives a stern disappointed look to Joel.

"Oh Jamie's just bringing the donor's labs to prove the liver is legit. Blockhead, you know him, right? He's bringing the liver shortly."

Joel continues to play a mixture of soul, jazz, and classic television theme songs for what seems like hours but is at most forty minutes. Then his phone vibrates. Joel smiles. At the same time, Ringo checks his phone and gives a confused look. Ringo silently removes himself from the studio. Joel's smile grows.

Blockhead arrives but he isn't alone, and the guy he has with him— a man in a suit the color of an Oingo Boingo song—is causing a big scene. He's claiming he has been summoned by Austein, but lobby security wasn't having it.

In the studio Joel stops playing. He attempts a humble and respectful posture as he approaches Austein.

"My man is in the building with the package."

Ringo exits the elevator into the lobby to speak with security.

"Ringo, you dumb mook. Since when do you speak for me? I'm here to see Austein."

Ringo walks past Cheddar who was spewing a string of insults. Ringo speaks only to Blockhead. The two large figures share short words above Cheddar and walk to the elevator. Ringo motions for Cheddar to follow like one would call for a dog. Cheddar chases behind them, stomping like an angry child.

In the studio, the medical staff is readying Austein. Dr. Manny and Dr. Jamie are taking inventory of their instruments.

Joel flits about the suite, excited and tense.

The studio door swings open hard yet silently. In the doorway stands Cheddar flanked by Ringo and Blockhead. His face goes through configurations of irritation, anger, confusion, and finally realization and fear. Cheddar sees Austein, who has supposedly summoned him in reference to Joel's debt. He sees Joel, who for some reason is near giddy. Then he sees Dr. Manny and Dr. Jamie, the two men he's been blackmailing. Though he had never met them in person, and he had only ever thought of them as "some married fag" and "the other fag," they were the two men he had been running through the ringer by holding over them evidence of their affair.

"Your liver is here Mr. Austein," Joel says bluntly.

Cheddar turns to run but is hoisted up off the ground by Ringo and Blockhead. Joel walks over and begins to pat him down. He removes a small black book from Cheddar's jacket pocket.

Ringo and Blockhead carry Cheddar over to an operating table where Jamie and Manny are ready to get to work. Dr. Manny with grace and finesse injects Cheddar with a sedative.

Joel flips through the black book. The first half contains gambling notes. Joel finds his page and tears it out. In the back of the book are rows and columns that look like a payment schedule. The table is labeled "FRUITS." Joel takes these pages and hands the book to Blockhead.

"Every degenerate that owes Cheddar now owes you. Except for me. That should cover your fee."

Blockhead takes the book and nods.

Jaimie and Manny are making quick time, already elbow deep in Cheddar's abdomen. Jamie looks to Joel. They share a look of brotherly love. Then Jamie looks to Manny and the two doctors look happy and relieved.

To no one in particular Joel speaks, "Jamie and Manny are out from under Cheddar's thumb, Austein's getting his liver, my debt is clear, and Blockhead is paid. Am I forgetting something?"

Ringo laughed, "You got anything in that bag for me?"

"I just made you the man who saved a king, Ringo. That's all I got."

SASHI

JOSHUA BRITTON

FOR MONTHS after he was abducted, James had thought little else about rebellion, but now he forced such thoughts from his mind. On this night he entered the dining hall, sheet music in hand, to find that he was to play not simply for The Man's private dinner—his usual evening task—but for a small party. His duties, however, were the same for a party as for a private dinner: he was expected to be practiced, prepared, and on call; expected to wear a suit when summoned; and expected to make music only, and not to talk.

At the piano this evening James played the hits of Mozart, Beethoven, and Debussy mixed in with some lesser-known composers of the baroque, classical, and romantic periods. Many he played from memory, like Schumann's "Arabesque," Grieg's "Butterfly," Chaminade's "Pierrette," several of the Bach inventions, and the first movement of Haydn's D major sonata, though he kept the sheet music out for the sonata's second and third movements. The guests split their attention between the music, small talk, and requests for refills from the waitstaff.

After an hour, he stood to take a short break. Dinner hadn't been served yet; the cocktail hour was taking a long time, though the guests didn't seem impatient. He took a moment to observe everyone. It was only a party of four, not counting James and the waitstaff. One of the guests stood as James was about to pass by him.

"Very fine work, James," the guest said. "I'm enjoying your playing very much. It's a treat."

James had been instructed, if pressed, to say as little as possible. A "thank you" would have sufficed. But he observed that The Man had momentarily stepped out, and that the other two guests were engaged with each other some feet away.

"I'm being held here against my will," James told him in a mezzo piano. "I need help. Please help me."

And he quickly made his exit. In the green room, he splashed water on his face and washed his hands as he willed his pounding heart to calm. He was as surprised by what he had said as he knew the guest must have been. He hadn't allowed the guest time to respond, so he couldn't gauge his reaction. He didn't even know if he'd been heard correctly and understood. James was not a brave man, normally, and part of him hoped that nothing would come of this.

He sipped some water, both relieved and disappointed that he was not being interrupted. After a time he left the green room to take back his place at the piano. Upon re-entering the dining hall, the room was silent, and everyone looked at him.

"James," The Man said to him. "My dear friend here—our guest, James, your guest as well as mine—says you told him something very odd a moment ago."

"Sir?" James said.

"You told me," the guest said, "that you are being held here against your will. That you need help."

"Is that what you said, James?" The Man said.

"Indeed it is, sir," James said, raising his voice to mask his wavery and nervous tone. He turned to address the entire quartet. "I have a bracelet on my ankle that shocks me something fierce if I get too close to the edge of the property. I am prohibited from leaving."

"An ankle bracelet," The Man repeated.

"Yes, sir," James said. "Shall I pull up my pant leg to show everyone?"

"James is employed as a musician in my home," The Man said to his guests. "A very fine pianist, I've always thought. He is provided room and board. I don't understand this joke. James," he said, turning to the pianist. "I want everybody to hear me say that you are not bound in any way. You are free to leave at any time, although, this odd joke aside, I hope you will continue. What do you say, James?"

James looked at The Man and at each of his three guests.

"I would like to continue in this position, sir, if you'll keep me. I apologize for my bizarre sense of humor."

He sat back down and offered to take requests. The guests suggested "Some Enchanted Evening" and "Night Train," and The Man asked for the three Gershwin preludes. Nobody asked him to pull up his pant leg. At the end of the evening, after everyone else had left, he was locked in his quarters. For several days he was fed only dry toast and water.

THE FIRST TIME he'd been punished in this manner came after their third dinner together. In a fit of defiance, James had sat on his hands and refused to play any longer. He had thought, naively, that if he didn't perform his sole function for being there, then he would be thrown back into society, like an undersized fish back into the water. But he wasn't thrown back. Henchmen entered the dining hall and led him away. A week later, he was released. After that, he performed as was expected.

"I enjoy a good rag, James."

Nine times out of ten it was just the two of them, as it was now, other than the entering and exiting waitstaff. Except for show in front of company, however, The Man hadn't previously spoken to James directly; before he'd always communicated his requests—his orders—by messenger. James's insubordination at the dinner party had not been acknowledged beyond his forced solitude.

"Thank you for obliging me," The Man said. "But I didn't recognize that last rag."

James smiled, eager for camaraderie. "'La Pas La Ma,'" he said. "Ernest Hogan, 1895. An early one."

"Before that you played 'The Entertainer,' obviously, and if I'm not mistaken, the 'Pineapple Rag?'"

"Very good, sir!"

The Man nodded, accepting the compliment. "I think I'd prefer it if you stuck to Joplin."

The Man spoke without expression but displayed an authoritative look in his eyes, and despite his passive wording James knew that he didn't have a choice. When he had requested Joplin in a message relayed to James earlier in the day, James had interpreted "Joplin" as ragtime in general. If he had told him "La Pas La Ma" was Joplin, he doubted The Man would have known the difference.

"Yes, sir," James complied.

He turned back to the keyboard and played "Elite Syncopations" and "The Maple Leaf Rag" as The Man slowly chewed his food, listening intently. Despite The Man's power display, James decided to build on their friendly banter. It was just the two of them, the help out of sight until summoned. The Man sat twenty feet away, alone at a large and thick mahogany dining table. With another rare bout of courage, James spoke.

"Sir," he began. "May I ask you a question?"

The Man didn't say anything, nor did he provide any physical indicator beyond an intense stare. But he didn't say no, either.

"This is a beautiful home, sir, and the grounds are gorgeous and meticulously kept. It's a joy to be here, sir, and I am grateful for the work. It's hard to find full-time work as a performer, and I don't take my good fortune for granted. I do wonder, though, sir, if I might be free to come and go from the premises, provided of course I continue with my duties in a thorough manner as I'm sure you will agree I have done thus far."

James had never spoken so formally, and he felt confident about what he'd said. But The Man still didn't speak. A few seconds passed. They felt like ages. Then The Man put down his knife and fork, stood up, and left the room. James was locked in his room and for several days he was fed only toast, without butter or jam, and given only water to drink.

THE COUNTRY had been a few weeks away from a controversial presidential election when James had been abducted, and it had seemed likely that one half of the country or the other was going to revolt, depending on the outcome. But in the months that had passed since his arrival at the mansion, James hadn't even seen a newspaper. Nor did he have access to a television or computer. He was in a bubble. During his rests he listened to the banter during The Man's occasional dinner parties, hoping for clues as to what was happening in the rest of the world, whether a civil war had broken out, or even who had won the World Series. But he learned nothing. From the bubble's many acres on the hill he could see nothing but vast lawns, budding gardens, and trees. He looked up to the sky, an occasional passing jumbo jet the only evidence of an outside world, other than his memory, which was rapidly growing more and more blurry— what were the names of his former neighbors, for instance, and what had they looked like?

A new woman was brought onto the premises. James was instructed to call her Debra, implying that the previous Debra, to whom he had never spoken or gotten to know, must have been discarded. It occurred to James only now that Debra wasn't the old Debra's real name. Of course, James wasn't his real name, either, though what he used to be called was becoming fuzzy.

"These are what criminals wear when they're under house arrest," the new Debra said to James. "So that if you run off, they can track you down and put you in jail."

She'd been in a funk ever since she arrived. Until now, shell-shocked just as James had been, she hadn't spoken a word to anyone. James took it upon himself to show her the grounds.

"It's more than a tracker," James said of the ankle bracelet. "It shocks you. And it hurts."

She shook her head in disbelief. "Like we're animals," she said.

"Exactly," James agreed. "Four houses down from me in the neighborhood where I grew up lived a dog named Sashi. Sashi was outside almost all of the time. She was a nice dog, gentle and lovable, and I would pet her every time I walked by. But she wore this same kind of shocker around her collar. See, there was an invisible fence that surrounded the perimeter of their yard, and if Sashi got too close to the edge, it would give her a shock and she'd jump back a few feet. If she somehow got even closer, she got an even bigger shock. To passersby, Sashi looked like an extraordinarily well-behaved dog who never left her unfenced yard. But there was a force field keeping her there."

Debra looked like she'd been shocked, though they were far from the perimeter.

"Where is this fence, exactly?" she asked.

James looked around. "Between those two trees," he said, pointing several yards ahead. "And it goes all the way around. The estate is sixty-four acres, so I can't say exactly where. But there's a buzzing sound when you get close, warning you that you're about to get zapped."

"And you've been zapped?"

He nodded.

"How bad was it?"

"It depends how close you get, and how long you stay there."

"What I'm wondering is," Debra said, "what if you run really hard, like a sprint, and take the pain for those few seconds, and come out the other side free as a bird."

Debra appeared more athletic than he was, but James shook his head anyway. "I had the same idea, but it knocked me down, and I couldn't walk for days."

He had built up a brisk jog, and he had figured, aided by the natural momentum of running downhill, that he would get to the other side with, as Debra had put it, only a few seconds of pain. How close he had come he did not know; he only vaguely remembered being picked up and carted back inside. He was not a tough person, but he didn't think anyone stronger than him would have been able to withstand the charge either. He hadn't been able to walk for days, maybe a week. He hadn't been able to do anything else, either—eat, speak, or control his bowels.

But Debra hadn't given up on the idea. She stared ahead of them, beyond where the invisible fence must end, fixed on escaping. She was listening intently. James knew her next question before she even asked—

"Is there a road there?"

If there was a road, it was hidden. But James had heard, beyond the trees and the hedge, the occasional faint sound of a vehicle driving by. It stood to reason that if cars passed by, a pedestrian might walk by as well.

"Help!" Debra screamed. "We're trapped! Help!"

"Stop," James urged her with a hiss. "You'll get electrocuted."

She ignored him and shrieked a few more pleas before he saw her startle. "Ow!" She took stock of herself, and, after finding herself still intact, looked at James as if he were a wimp. "That's what you're afraid of?" And she went on hollering.

"It gets worse, I'm telling you," James said, less confident than before. It was clear that Debra was stronger than him, but how much stronger he was beginning to wonder.

There was another hiccup in her yelling. James assumed she'd been zapped again. But she continued on. There were so many trees that it would be easy to hide dozens of cameras on the grounds, and James was sure they were being watched. He looked around, helplessly, hoping that whoever was watching them recognized that he'd been discouraging Debra from doing this.

Her yelling stopped abruptly, more than a hiccup this time. James turned to see that Debra had fallen backwards and was convulsing on the ground. James expected henchmen to come grab her and carry her back to the mansion, as had happened to him. But she twitched for half a minute, then lay still a little longer, seemingly conscious.

"And it gets even worse than that," James said, unsympathetically, once it was clear that she was all right.

She sat up, scared again. "This is inhumane," she whimpered. "What are we going to do?"

James shrugged. "Can you walk?" He held out his hand to assist her up, but she batted it away and stood on her own.

BY REQUEST, James was playing "Night and Day," "Fly Me to the Moon," and other selections from the Great American Songbook, while The Man and Debra sat several feet away dining on Cornish game hen. James was permitted to eat whatever was in the kitchen, and when he finished playing, the staff would prepare for him whatever they had prepared for The Man. Usually he ate simply, prepared his own sandwiches, not wanting to create extra work for the help who, he assumed, were held against their will as he was. But, as he played "I've Got a Crush On You," he thought he might splurge tonight.

Debra wore a sequined red evening gown. James had seen her rotate through several dresses during her dates with The Man over the weeks. She wore makeup, too, on these dates, though she didn't otherwise. The Man would glance at her every few bites, and Debra would force a quick smile, a smile that vanished the second The Man glanced away. James shook his head. It was best not to think about it. Yes, Cornish game hen sounded good.

He played on and tried not to think of the happy couple. As far as incarcerations went, things certainly could be worse. He was welcome to the twelve-foot Steinway in the dining hall whenever the dining hall wasn't in use. The Steinway was one of the finest instruments he'd ever played on. During the times when he was told to stay out of certain rooms, including the dining hall, he could use a quality Baldwin upright in his quarters. From the Baldwin's piano bench he had a nice view of the gardens, a view the dining hall lacked. There was a third piano, too, a baby grand in the parlor of the east wing, which he often forgot about. All three pianos were impeccably maintained, though he never saw a tuner or technician. His job was made clear—to provide the music, *not* to ask questions, and certainly not to complain.

Debra's job was to provide comfort for The Man. James wondered if she was required to provide comfort for anyone else. Debra was the closest thing he had to a friend here, and he was reasonably confident it was mutual. The mansion was huge, and he didn't see her every day, sometimes not for several days in a row. But when he did see her, she was civil, and they walked the grounds together, though they did not always talk.

He finally mustered the courage to knock on her door. He hadn't seen her in two days, not since a delicious vegan pasta dinner two nights earlier; James had helped himself to the leftovers. She opened the door, and James thought she was perhaps relieved he wasn't someone else. James hadn't been in her quarters before, but could see that, while his quarters were an apartment consisting of a bedroom, private bathroom, and sitting room with a piano, she only had a bedroom.

Debra stood and waited. James held up a single rose that he'd cut from the garden that afternoon.

"You're not coming in here," she said.

James had been smiling, but his smile faded as he softly nodded in agreement. His finger began to bleed from one of the thorns on the stem.

"I know what you're after, but you won't find it here," she said, closing the door.

Dejected, he walked the east wing and the common areas—the west wing was forever off limits. The loneliness got to him. Employees were everywhere, but he was near-universally ignored. He would stand just outside the kitchen, listening to the workers comingle and gossip, trying to learn anything—where exactly they were, who exactly The Man was, and whether or not he, James, was actually safe. The second he walked into the kitchen, the whispering stopped. The grounds crew ignored him, as well, though they didn't talk to each other either. Sometimes he thought he could hear screams coming through the vents and air ducts from the nether regions of the mansion, though he wasn't sure if it wasn't just his imagination. He'd walk the hallways, sometimes stopping at a door, debating whether or not to open it, wondering if behind it there was a secret stairway that led to a torture chamber.

Otherwise, he was given notes, either slipped under his door or handed to him during his walks by an emotionless servant, notes pertaining to what was expected of him today, tomorrow, or this week. Except for the occasional compliment, The Man didn't engage James in conversation, even though half of the time it was just the two of them in the room.

He would play half a dozen nocturnes, preludes, mazurkas, and waltzes. Then The Man, having finished with his meal, would stand up. "Very good, James," he'd say. "I enjoy Chopin. Well done." Then The Man would leave, and James would gather his sheet music while somebody from the kitchen entered to clear the table.

Who were these people? And where had they come from? Why didn't more revolt? Surely they weren't all prisoners like Debra and himself. His memory of his hapless escape attempt was uncertain, but he knew someone had to have pulled him out of the electric field, someone who did not have an ankle bracelet, someone not confined within the same boundaries, someone who was not The Man. And the doctor who nursed him back to health—was he trapped, too? James hadn't seen the doctor since. Some of them had to be civilians, though The Man would need enormous confidence in his vetting system to allow somebody to come and go.

He liked to think that the waitstaff held secret meetings at odd hours in remote hallways and closets, plotting escape. Nobody invited him, which bothered him; when the time came to bolt he hoped to tag along. He didn't know anybody. While he talked to Debra, he didn't actually *know* her. They never talked about escaping, not a second time, not since she'd been knocked backwards at the edge.

Would the staff dare talk about it? He assumed that there were cameras everywhere in the mansion, but were there also microphones?

He knocked on her door. He'd knocked earlier that day but hadn't gotten a response. That didn't mean anything. He imagined that she was so full of self-loathing after an evening with The Man that she couldn't bear to see or talk to anyone. The only peace she got was when she had her period, the only time The Man would leave her alone for a few days, although even then he'd send somebody to examine her and make sure she wasn't lying.

Finally she opened her door.

"No roses this time," James said, holding his hands up defensively, chuckling.

Debra's room was dim, but a blade of light from the hall lamp cut across her face and he saw that she was badly bruised, her eye sockets swollen.

"Oh, geez," James said. "What happened?"

Debra didn't say anything, but glared at him, her eyes saying, "What do you think happened?" And James knew that she'd rebelled— had a fit of defiance, had objected to being touched in a certain way—and that The Man had retaliated.

James only stared, tongue-tied.

"There's nothing you can do," Debra said. "So don't even ask."

She was giving him the benefit of the doubt, he appreciated, that he might have had the courage to stick up for her, to fight for her. He'd known a dozen better classical pianists than himself in his previous life, and another dozen better jazz pianists, though nobody he knew had been as good a doubler. But it was likely he'd been targeted not solely for his piano skills, but also for his cowardice, lacking the will to act.

"What can I do?" he stupidly forced out.

"Don't even pretend," she said as she shut the door.

LIFE COULD BE WORSE, he thought, a life which consisted primarily of four activities: eat, sleep, piano, R&R. For R&R he could walk the grounds or read— The Man had a vast library, though nothing written in the last thirty years, and James was welcome to read anything in it. But his perks were limited. For instance, while he'd never been overly athletic, there were times that he would have liked somebody with whom to toss a ball around. His only other real complaint was that his life lacked intimacy. It would have been nice to be touched, though he wouldn't say this out loud, especially not to Debra.

Debra kept to herself, and James saw her only once or twice a week. Many months had passed since her black eye. She may have been given more, for all he knew. It had only taken James a few weeks to break down and accept the inevitable. It seemed that Debra, more than a year in, still refused to do so.

They were strolling the lawns and gardens and he wasn't paying attention to where they were going until Debra stopped and he realized they were at the perimeter, in full view of the hedge so many yards ahead.

"You won't make it," James said. "It's too strong. It might even kill you."

"I can't live like this anymore," she said. "Death would be better."

"I'm sure if you asked you could do something different here. There are plenty of maids. What's one more?"

"A maid? Christ, James, you have no idea how good you have it. You're a goddam pianist. Of course you're content!"

She grabbed ahold of his hand, their first actual physical contact, and in fact, James realized, the first time he'd been touched by anybody since he had been nursed back to health after his electrocution.

"What do you think would happen to you if your fingers stopped working?" she said, tightening her grip on his hand. "Would he make you a butler? If you lost your hand in an accident?

He tried to pull his hand away, but her grasp was too firm. She was the closest he had to a friend; surely she wouldn't intentionally injure him. But he hadn't seen her this way before. Morose plenty of times, but never this determined.

"I'm going for it," she said. She released his hand, and he rubbed his wrist where her grip had left marks and begun to hurt. She'd probably been thinking about this for days, or even weeks, psyching herself into it.

She'd be running downhill, she had certainly taken into consideration, so that even if the power of the electricity knocked her down, she might continue rolling if she fell the right way.

She looked at James, and James expected an invitation. Instead, she said, "Nice knowing you."

She got into position, like she'd once been a trained sprinter.

"Debra, don't," James said, reaching out to put his hand on her shoulder.

She rapidly turned, grabbed hold of his left wrist with both of her hands, yanked, and twisted. James fell to the ground and yelped in pain, unable to move his fingers. He cried and wailed and screamed. Debra looked at him, disgusted. And then she ran.

Fighting through the groaning and moaning, he yelled after her, "Don't do it, Deb, stop!" The pain was excruciating, and he felt like he was going to pass out.

Debra hit the fence and James heard the electricity surge. Her sprint turned into flails. After a few more steps she fell to the ground, shaking and flopping like a fish thrown ashore. James saw how ridiculous he must have looked when he had tried.

The loud buzz of electricity persisted, but she kept moving, rolling, pushing herself. When James had tried this, he'd soiled himself by now. Like watching a spider being flushed down the toilet, James found himself rooting for her. Debra herself didn't make a sound.

She rolled on. James's vision was blurry from his wrist pain, but he could still make her out. Her arms and legs keep pushing her forward.

"Debra," he moaned, helplessly. Because he was with her, and because they had fraternized, he expected to be punished more ruthlessly than ever before, and interrogated, like the family of a North Korean defector. But her freedom could be worth it, he thought, particularly if she later sent for help, and if someone came for him.

The buzzing stopped. She was through! She tried to stand up but couldn't quite. Still, when she fell, she fell forward. She pulled herself upright with the aid of a tree. James remained writhing on the ground, holding his wrist, bent at a right angle. His future, his purpose for being, it dawned on him, was wholly dependent on his hands.

Debra glanced back for the first time, hair frizzy, arms, legs, and neck twitching. Did she feel remorse for hurting him so badly? She looked at him in horror. Because of guilt? But no, she wasn't looking at him, but beyond him. James turned his head to see several henchmen barreling down the hill. Debra took off, running as best she could in zigzags, banging into trees and bouncing off of them as if she were a pinball.

The men ran past James, dismissing him as a low flight risk. Debra crawled through a tiny gap in the hedge and disappeared. The men closed in behind. One of them tried following Debra through the gap, while the others raced to go around the long way.

James had often imagined that he could hear cars or trucks driving by in the distance, though a road wasn't visible, not even in the winter when the trees were bare. But now tires screeched to a stop—the road must exist after all!—and he heard what sounded like a small crash. In desperation, Debra must have run into the road to stop the car. The driver must have braked too late and slammed Debra into the windshield.

And then there was silence. James couldn't see anything, and he'd forgotten to whimper. He turned his head around but there wasn't anyone behind him. Even though he was lying on the ground, there was nothing wrong with his legs and he figured he should get up and seek a physician.

He heard yelling. He couldn't make out any words, but there were several voices. The yelling was brief, though, interrupted by several gun shots. Then all was silent again, and he knew that Debra and the driver were no more.

HE WAS ASKED questions but wasn't otherwise tortured. His wrist was reset and bandaged. While his wrist healed, he was confined to his quarters. When they let him out for exercise, he walked the grounds, breathing in the fresh air, trying not to recall the events surrounding his broken wrist. He sensed that he was under constant though distant supervision; a gardener, for instance, seemed to pay more attention to him than to the garden. Meals were delivered to his quarters, but instead of dry toast he was served gourmet meals; for one dinner he even received Cornish game hen.

One early evening, during a storm, the wind knocked the power out. James was in his quarters, presumably locked in, though he'd stopped checking the door. From outside he heard commotion, and when he looked through the window he saw several figures sprinting in the waning daylight toward the edge of the property. They were followed by a second group of figures. James lost sight of them in the shadows of the trees. Then he heard multiple guns unloading at once. The food service wasn't up to par for several days after.

Over the years several Debras came and went, arriving and disappearing without fanfare. He rarely spoke to them.

His wrist seemed to take ages to heel, and he worried that The Man would grow impatient with the healing process, find a new musician, and dispose of him. But eventually he resumed playing for dinners, private and not, though his left wrist couldn't keep up with his right anymore. He contented himself with less challenging repertoire, music he'd been taught in middle and high school. With every passing Debra, he came to feel more and more grateful to The Man for keeping him on. He would tell him so, in short, curt, expressionless phrases, which The Man allowed.

In middle age, he kept coming back to the dog. So much of his former life had grown hazy or had been forgotten, but in his memory Sashi remained as vivid as ever. By the time James was getting ready to go to college, she didn't move as energetically as she once had. And there were times later in her life, he remembered, when Sashi wandered outside the boundaries of her electric fence. He would find her on the apron of the lawn, between the sidewalk and street, or she'd be lying down in her neighbor's yard. The batteries in her collar were dead, or perhaps the collar had been turned off. Occasionally she wasn't even wearing the collar; her family hadn't put it back on after her bath.

But she never ran away, never went farther than the neighbor's yard. Nor did she go in the road. Ten feet beyond the electric fence was all the change of scenery she was interested in. She knew where her home was, where she was safe, and who would provide for her. And young James would kneel down next to her and scratch her behind her ears, and she'd roll over for a belly rub. And then he'd be on his way, and she'd watch him go, silently sitting just outside of her allotted boundary.

From the mansion James stepped onto the grass and walked down the hill. He had replayed the fateful day in his mind thousands of times. This was where Debra had fallen the first time, and this was where she had begun to crawl and to tuck-and-roll. This was the hedge she had crawled through, the hedge several feet taller now, and thicker. James was too old now to get on his hands and knees and try crawling through it. He walked the length of the hedge, looking for a gap large enough to walk through.

On the other side of the hedge now, he reversed direction. This was where Debra had come through to the other side, no longer able to run in a straight line. The road was close, no more than twenty feet from the hedge. She could barely stand. This is where she must have run out into the road, where she got hit by the car, and where the henchmen caught up to her. They tried reasoning with the unlucky driver, James imagined, trying to convince him that what he was seeing wasn't what it seemed, before deciding to simply shoot him, and Debra as well.

He liked to think that if Debra had made it she would have sent help, that he would have been rescued. But what about The Man? Would he really have sat pat waiting for SWAT to bust everyone out? Or would he have destroyed the evidence, including James, and fled? It was probably best for James that Debra hadn't made it.

How many years, James wasn't sure, but it had been so long. His hair was gray and thin now, and he moved slower than he used to. He no longer knew what the world looked like. He didn't know who was still out there, what new inventions had become all the rage, who the president was, or if baseball had expanded. Behind him, in the mansion, he had a job. He had a home and people to look after him. For years he'd been keeping an ear out for whisperings of a new James. But it would be harder to find someone to play the piano than to find someone who could make a bed. James clung to that thought.

Sometimes they would forget to reattach his ankle bracelet after his baths. Like Sashi, he was free to roam. On the far side of the hedge, it was silent. No sirens or alarms. No yelling or thumping of running footsteps. No buzzing electricity. Was anybody even watching anymore?

A car was coming; he heard it before he saw it. James held up his hand to smile and wave. The car didn't slow down, didn't stop. James stood idly by, gazing after it, watching it shrink down the road. Cars looked different now. When it was gone, he turned around to head back up the hill. It would be dinner time soon, and he was expected to play.

LIKE YOU MEAN IT

DANIEL W. WRIGHT

VICTOR GRUBB sat at the piano on stage at Keys', the jazz club he had a residency at every Wednesday, Thursday, and Friday. A lit cigarette burned away in his hand while he was lost in thought.

Victor had learned to play piano at an early age, at the insistence of a Baptist grandmother who believed left-handedness was a gateway to Hell. At eight, his mother insisted that his grandmother stop on account that she kept telling him he was going to Hell. At thirteen, he picked it up again after seeing a Marx Brothers film and watched Chico playing with his "shoot the keys" style while giving flirtatious glances at the lady sitting next to him. For him, playing the piano became a party trick. Until his grandfather passed. His grandfather was a fan of the *Great American Songbook* and he learned many of the songs, not to perform, but to feel like his grandfather was still around. When Victor had been younger, his grandfather would put on a Frank Sinatra or Nat King Cole record and stare at the scotch he poured like it was telling him the weather. His favorite song had been "Misty" and Victor learned it in two days. In his mid-twenties, he began playing around to make extra money and enjoy the occasional hook-up. Twenty years and a divorce later, at 47, he played for the same reasons, and for people who shouted over them about parking or crypto or Taylor Swift tickets. His playing had improved, but the audience had not.

Keys' was a club in name only. It was really a dying restaurant with a piano and a lighting rig held together by wishful thinking. The only thing jazz about it was the way the menu changed without warning and the waitstaff made up prices depending on their mood.

Victor looked down at the cigarette in his hand. He didn't remember lighting it. He rarely did anymore. He put it out and looked at the clock. 4:45. In a little over three hours he'd start his first set. His sets were a mixture of jazz standards, 60s and 70s pop hits for the older martini crowd, and some late 90s and early 2000s for the wine mom crowd. Victor hoped someone would request something before they were two martinis deep and shouted for "Piano Man," the "Freebird" of all piano players. But more likely, they'd just talk over him again. Unless something unexpected happened.

The heavy requests for "Piano Man" would usually come around 10:30 or 11:00, when the crowds were drunk enough that he would receive as many as five requests for it a minute. So much so that he began to take pride in not caring to know how to play it. But after enough customers complained, and the owner of the club made it clear that he'd lose his gig if he didn't play the song, Victor was suddenly all too happy to play Billy Joel's signature tune.

He wound up playing it three times a night, sometimes four if someone slipped him a ten. He played it passive-aggressively, like a man performing CPR on a mannequin he hated. He changed keys for no reason. He sang it in the voice of a cartoon dog. One night he played the melody with only his pinky finger while eating onion rings with the other hand. People loved it.

The humiliation of it was strangely liberating. He was no longer a pianist. He was a clown with a piano. A court jester with a tip jar.

IT WAS JUST PAST ELEVEN when Ellis Penrose sat down at the far end of the bar, wearing his usual too-tight blazer and too-sincere smile. Victor had played for oil lobbyists, yoga moms, and guys who called jazz "vintage lo-fi." But Ellis? Ellis was something else.

Ellis had never known a life without. His family was upper-class, though they liked to think of themselves as middle-class. Ellis had never done anything unduly cruel. In fact, he was a loyal friend, the kind who'd literally give you the shirt off his back. And yet, he was still the kind of person a jaded man might want to punch on general principle. It wouldn't be right. It wouldn't be fair. But it would feel amazing. And somehow... cosmically justified.

A week earlier, over a tenth IPA he didn't need, Ellis had tried impressing Lena—a regular who freelanced as a consultant for startup founders and the occasionally morally flexible politician. He'd had his eye on her for months. Lena was everything he wanted in someone: good-looking (their hypothetical kids, in his opinion, would be devastatingly attractive), intelligent, sociable, driven, and financially independent enough that he wouldn't have to worry about losing all of his money if they divorced.

On top of that, she was nice. Not performatively so—genuinely kind in a way that made him feel seen. Whenever he spotted her, he'd slip into his best impression of Jon Hamm in a cologne commercial. This, in his mind, was the ultimate seduction strategy. And to be fair, it had worked more often than it should've.

LENA SAW RIGHT through it, of course. But his theatrics amused her in a "this is free content" kind of way. Which is why, emboldened by hops and self-delusion, Ellis had told her—completely sincerely—that he could not only play piano, but also compose songs "on instinct—like Mozart with anxiety."

Lena sat at a table near the stage with her best friend, Melanie (Victor's ex-wife), and Melanie's husband, Todd, who had the confident, oblivious aura of a man who didn't know how many people secretly hated him.

Victor and Melanie's marriage had been a brief and ill-advised detour in their mid-twenties. For all the similarities they clung to during their six-month courtship, they discovered every incompatibility the moment they got engaged. But instead of breaking it off, they played a game of matrimonial chicken—and lost.

The result was a two-year war of attrition held together by sarcasm, alcohol, and hate-fucking so intense that both of them ended up in therapy when it finally collapsed.

All these years later, one thing remained constant: Melanie's belief that Victor could be something if he ever really tried. After their split, Melanie met a man named Todd. Victor didn't think much of Todd—but then, not many people did. Still, he had to admit: Todd and Melanie fit. And even though it had been nearly twenty years since their marriage ended, her happiness still mattered to him more than he liked to admit.

While Victor played, Lena asked Ellis about his songwriting talents. At first, he looked confused—until the drunken idiocy from a week prior began to dawn on him. Desperate to impress her, he doubled down.

"Of course," Ellis said, nodding with the swagger of a man bluffing a poker hand with a two and a napkin. "I can write a song."

Melanie and Todd, confused at first, quickly caught on and watched the exchange with barely concealed amusement.

"Write one about me," Lena said, eyes gleaming with mischief.

Ellis leaned forward, thinking this was his golden opportunity. "Sure thing. Give me a week—I'll come up with something."

"Something," Lena repeated, feigning offense. "A song about me would just be something?"

"No, I mean—" Ellis scrambled, "I'll come up with something great."

"Aww, thank you," Lena said sweetly.

"Can I get you a drink?" Ellis asked, eager to change the subject before she pushed the bluff any further.

"Glass of Malbec," she said.

As Ellis left for the bar, Melanie leaned in. "What's going on?"

"Just his usual shit," Lena replied.

"What if he actually writes something?"

"If he gets anywhere near the truth, we'll talk. Until then?" Lena smiled. "Guilty until proven innocent."

AT 1:30, VICTOR was done for the night. Joan, the bartender, slid a beer down the bar toward him. It wasn't much of a feat—maybe four feet of laminate—but Victor liked the idea of it. A bartender sliding him a drink made him feel like he was in some dive in a Raymond Chandler novel run by Humphrey Bogart in Casablanca.

"Hey, maestro."

Victor turned to see Melanie approaching the bar, Lena just a step behind her. Both had the look of people who were slightly buzzed but still fully in control—Melanie with her arms crossed and eyebrows raised, Lena with that easy, unreadable smile that always made Victor feel like he was about to be gently roasted.

"You were great tonight," Melanie said. "Almost made me forget I used to fantasize about setting your keyboard on fire."

Victor gave her a half-smile. "And yet, you never did. Restraint becomes you."

Melanie snorted and looked to Lena. "Tell him."

Lena leaned forward against the bar, chin resting on one hand. "You were wonderful, Victor. That medley in the second set? Gorgeous."

Victor felt his chest tighten slightly, the way it sometimes did when she looked at him like that—like he mattered.

"Thanks," he said, trying not to sound too sincere. "Been practicing for twenty-five years straight. Might finally get the hang of it someday."

Lena laughed, and Melanie shot her a look that Victor couldn't read. He glanced at Lena again—too long, maybe. There was something magnetic about her, something playful and sharp that had always drawn his eye.

But he never pursued it. She was Melanie's friend. And that felt like a can of worms soaked in lighter fluid.

"Well," Melanie said, brushing something invisible off her coat, "we're heading out. Don't get yourself into any trouble."

"No promises," Victor said.

Lena gave him one last smile before following Melanie toward the door. "Goodnight, Victor."

"Night," he said.

And just like that, they were gone. But there was still one person left.

Ellis sat alone at the far end of the bar, nursing an Old Fashioned and typing into his phone with the intense, delusional focus of a man who thought he was writing a masterpiece. His blazer had somehow grown tighter over the course of the night. His expression was one Victor knew too well: that dangerous cocktail of alcohol, self-confidence, and a bad idea taking shape. Victor took another sip and sighed.

When Ellis looked up and saw Victor, he got up and wandered over, footsteps soft against the worn wood floor. Victor looked up, startled—like a raccoon caught rifling through trash—then groaned as Ellis brightened.

"Just the guy I wanted to see!"

"Lucky me," Victor said.

Ellis shoved his drink aside like it was getting in the way of genius. "How long did it take you to learn piano?"

Victor raised an eyebrow. "Why?"

"Well, I was wondering if you could maybe help me write a song?"

Victor didn't answer. He'd heard this before—from trust-fund DJs, from marketing execs going through their midlife "creative era," from one guy who claimed jazz was just "musical improv with better lighting."

Ellis leaned in. "Like, we collaborate. You play, I write. Lennon and McCartney."

Victor rubbed his face like a migraine was circling. "Lennon and McCartney both worked at their craft for six years before they had a hit."

"Yeah, sure, but I've got ideas. I've got the feeling, you know?"

Victor glanced at the nearly empty bar. The buzz was fading. The headache was real.

"Look," said Victor, "I don't have time to teach someone how to play piano, let alone co-write with a guy who probably only ever wrote expense reports."

"What if I made it worth your while?"

Victor turned. "I'm listening."

"Twenty thousand," Ellis said. "Cash. No bullshit."

"For?"

"Teaching me to play. Writing a song I can perform."

"I thought you wanted to co-write?"

"I think you'd be better at that stuff," Ellis said, with the honesty of someone who didn't realize how insulting he was being.

Victor didn't believe a drunken word that was coming out of Ellis' mouth. But he figured he may as well call his bluff.

"Twenty-five," Victor said. "Meet me at my place tomorrow."

"Oh, I can't do tomorrow. I've got a thing."

Victor rolled his eyes. "If you want me to do your homework, you're at least going to show up. To-morrow. Bring half the money so I know you're serious. You can pay me the other half when we're done."

"Okay," Ellis said, and stuck out his hand. Victor reluctantly shook it. Ellis started to walk away.

"Hey," Victor called after him.

Ellis turned. "Yeah?"

"Don't you want my address?"

"You're really not my type," Ellis said. Victor stared at him blankly. He saw Ellis remember what he was talking about, exclaiming, "Oh! Right. Yeah, that's probably a good idea."

Victor shook his head and scribbled it on the back of a business card. He handed it over.

"Four-thirty. Sharp. Be there."

Ellis took the card and wandered out like a man who'd just closed a business deal that involved no actual business.

When the last patron left, Victor climbed back onto the stage and played for the staff as they wiped tables and counted tips. He started into "Everything Happens to Me," a favorite he rarely performed for crowds. Someone always said it was too depressing. The only Chet Baker tune he could play with vocals was "Let's Get Lost." And no one ever requested that one either.

THE NEXT DAY, Victor sat at his portable piano, a glass of rye sweating next to a stack of fake books and a half-eaten granola bar that had become his lunch by accident. His apartment was a mix of tasteful disrepair and functional chaos—old records, dead plants, jazz posters curling at the corners. He plinked out a few chords, stopped, stared at the keys like they owed him money, and sighed.

He checked the clock: 4:28.

Then: 4:34.

Then: 4:43.

At 4:47, the buzzer rang. Victor didn't move right away—he just stared at the door like it might apologize. He considered ignoring it. Make Ellis sweat. Let him stew in his own entitled lateness. But then he remembered who he was dealing with. Ellis would just assume Victor wasn't home, shrug, and go get a latte. Maybe write a Medium post about how jazz is dead and it's capitalism's fault. Victor pressed the buzzer and unlocked the front door.

A minute later, Ellis appeared at the top of the stairs, wearing joggers, a puffy vest over a Henley, and the smug glow of a man who thought being "a few minutes late" was actually charming. He held a to-go coffee and a reusable bottle of flavored electrolyte water like he was between yoga and TED Talk auditions.

"Yo!" Ellis said, walking in like he'd been invited to a party. "Sorry—traffic was murder."

"You live six blocks away," Victor muttered.

Ellis blinked. "Still. Traffic. Uh, sorry, man."

Victor motioned to the piano. "You bring the money?"

Ellis pulled out an envelope and tossed it on the coffee table with a theatrical flourish, like he was on a game show.

Victor opened it, counted quickly. Twenty-five grand in neat hundreds. The bank teller probably thought he'd gotten in the drug trade.

"I said just bring half."

"Right. I just figured... front-loading might build trust," Ellis said, smiling.

Victor sighed. He wasn't wrong. "Sit."

Ellis did. Poorly. Like someone who had never sat at a piano and wasn't sure if it required core strength.

Victor handed him a basic exercise sheet. "Play that."

Ellis stared at the paper, flipped it upside down, then looked at Victor. "This is, uh... mostly squiggles."

"That's called notation."

"I feel like we're not acknowledging how subjective this all is."

Victor rubbed his temple. "Jesus Christ."

Ellis hesitated. "Okay, but—listen. I know I suck. I know I'm not, like, you. I just..."

He trailed off. Victor looked over.

"I just want to write something for this girl," Ellis said finally. "Not to sleep with her. I mean—I wouldn't complain. But really... I just want her to think I'm not full of shit. That there's something in me worth paying attention to. And something about her... just moves me. Like more than anything else. And I also think we'd look good together."

Victor studied him for a long moment.

"You know what the saddest thing about jazz is?" Victor said. Ellis shook his head.

"It's not that no one listens to it. It's that people only pretend to when they're trying to seem deep. But the music—it doesn't care. It's honest. You can't fake it."

Ellis paused. "I don't get it."

Victor sighed. "You want to impress her? Then don't fake it."

Ellis nodded slowly. "So... you'll help me?"

Victor sighed like a man boarding a plane he knew was going to crash.

"God help me. Yeah. Let's start with C major."

Ellis looked confused. "Is that... like... the normal one?"

Victor rolled his eyes. "It's the white keys. Don't get creative."

Ellis squinted at the keys.

"So... this is C?"

Victor nodded. "Middle C. It's like basecamp. Everything starts here."

Ellis poked it like it might bite. The note rang out, thin and isolated.

Victor grimaced. "Okay, now the rest of the scale. Just white keys, one finger."

Ellis began tentatively plinking upward, his index finger stiff like he was dialing an old rotary phone. When he hit the final note, he looked up, triumphant.

"I did it."

"You sounded like a grandparent typing a Yelp review."

"Yeah, but like… a musical grandparent."

Victor stood up. "No. Get up."

"What?"

"Stand. I'm playing it for you. You need to hear it right."

Ellis reluctantly stood, stretching like he'd just been asked to lift something heavier than his own ego. Victor sat down and played the scale, then again with a gentle swing, then again turning it into a little melodic riff.

"You hear the difference?" Victor asked.

Ellis nodded slowly. "Yours sounds like it means something."

"That's because I don't play like I'm afraid the keys are rigged to explode."

He motioned to the seat again. Ellis sat.

Victor exhaled. "Let's try chords."

"Is that like… multiple notes at once?"

"Yes," Victor said, deadpan. "Very good. Next week we learn what a 'song' is."

Ellis gave a sheepish grin. "Look, I know I'm terrible. I just figured—if anyone could help me fake my way into writing a love song, it's you."

Victor flinched. "I don't fake songs."

Ellis sobered. "Right. Sorry. I didn't mean it like that."

There was a long silence.

Ellis finally broke it. "It's just... I've never really made something before. Not that wasn't a pitch deck or a LinkedIn post. I guess I just want to know what it feels like. You know? To make something real. Something that says what I actually feel, even if it's a mess."

Victor glanced at him. For a second, Ellis didn't look like a rich idiot trying to cosplay authenticity— he looked like someone reaching for something he couldn't name.

It reminded Victor of himself, years ago, hunched over a cheap keyboard in a borrowed apartment, trying to turn heartbreak into melody.

"Alright," Victor said finally. "Here's the deal. You show up on time. You practice. You shut the hell up when I'm explaining something."

Ellis sat up straighter. "Deal."

Victor pointed at the keyboard. "Now play me a C chord. With your whole hand."

Ellis poised all five fingers like a toddler approaching finger paint. He pressed the keys. The chord rang out—clunky, uneven, but real.

Victor sighed.

"Good," he said. "Now do that nine thousand more times."

"But that's a lot," said Ellis.

"You want to impress someone, the labor shouldn't matter," said Victor. "It's the fact that you did it for them."

"That's beautiful," said Ellis.

"Yeah," muttered Victor. "It's fucking Shakespeare."

"Well, tell me about songwriting," said Ellis. "What's the thing to do… there."

"We're kinda getting ahead of ourselves there," said Victor.

"Well, just tell me the basics."

Victor rolled his eyes. "You like this girl?"

"Yeah."

"What does she make you feel?"

"I don't know."

"You love her so much but you don't know what she makes you feel?"

"She's just… really cool."

"Okay," said Victor. "That's a starting point. A seventh grade starting point, but a starting point nonetheless. Why is she cool?"

"She just is," said Ellis.

"So, dig deeper there," said Victor. "What was the first thing you noticed about her?"

"Honestly? Her tits."

"Okay," said Victor, biting his lip. "Maybe don't start there, but I appreciate the honesty. What else?"

"I guess…"

"I'm gonna stop you right there," said Victor. "Don't ever guess. If you don't know why you like this person, then do you even like them?"

"Yeah!"

"Why?"

"Because she's just fucking awesome!"

"Okay!" said Victor. "We've gone from seventh grade to ninth! I dig it. Let's keep going."

Ellis looked confused about what to do next. Victor leaned back. He looked at Ellis like a dog that had almost learned how to open the fridge: impressed, confused, and a little bit worried.

"You ever write a letter to someone?" Victor asked.

"Like… in cursive?"

Victor blinked. "Maybe. Just a letter. Like, an actual message. A letter. Not a DM, not a Snap. A letter. With words that mean something."

Ellis thought for a moment, then shook his head. "I think I once wrote a birthday card to my grandma?"

Victor exhaled sharply. "Jesus. All right. Hang on."

Victor got up and rifled through a warped wooden filing cabinet that doubled as a side table. From a folder tucked between old lead sheets and unpaid parking tickets, he pulled a yellowed notebook with frayed corners. The pages were soft and greasy from age and use.

Victor flipped to a dog-eared page and held it up without looking. "This," he said, "is what a love song looks like before you ruin it with production."

Ellis took the notebook like it might combust in his hands. He scanned the page, mouthing the words silently. The song was called "A Rose as Sweet." Victor tried to remember how the song started before he began singing.

A rose by any other name
Would still smell as sweet

And I'd still find you in the dark
By the shuffle of your feet

The words you say don't always rhyme
But they all sound like home
I'd trade my chords for just one note
That told me I'm not alone

You laugh like nothing's ever wrong
Your smile is always there
And loving you feels just the same
As breathing in the air

So call yourself a passing cloud
A ghost beneath the sheet
A rose by any other name
Would still smell as sweet

His brow lifted. "Whoa. This is really good."

"Thank you," said Victor dryly, settling back on the piano bench.

"You wrote this for someone?"

Victor nodded slowly. "A long time ago. She liked roses and Billie Holiday. She thought Chet Baker sounded like heartbreak in a suit. So I wrote her this."

"That's... damn, man. Could you perform that again?"

"Sure," said Victor. Ellis took out his phone and recorded Victor singing the song. Ellis heaped more praise upon Victor after the second performance. Ellis looked down at the lyrics.

"You mind if I, uh…" Ellis said, pointing toward his phone.

Victor was already looking away. "Knock yourself out."

Ellis snapped a picture, then one more, just to be sure. "Thanks, man. Seriously. This means a lot."

Victor grunted. "Don't thank me till you play something that doesn't make me want to swallow my own face.

Ellis smiled. "I think I'm gonna make this work."

Victor gave him a long, skeptical look. "That's what scares me."

Ellis packed up and left with a cheerful little wave. As the door closed, Victor looked down at the keys. He plunked out the first chord of the song. Then he said, to no one in particular, "Shit."

TWO WEEKS LATER, Keys' was fuller than usual for a Thursday. Something about the humidity made people nostalgic, willing to sit in a dim room filled with strangers and watch someone try to be somebody.

Victor was already at the bar, glass of rye in hand, tapping his foot against the stool leg. He had just finished his first set and was glad to unwind for the next forty-five minutes before his second set.

While Victor had been performing, Lena asked Ellis at the bar about the song he had promised to write her. Ellis had written the lyrics to "A Rose as Sweet" in his handwriting and shown it to Lena. She was touched.

"I'll be singing this for you tonight," he said, as smooth as possible.

In truth, Ellis had taken the footage of Victor and gone to another piano teacher and paid him to teach Ellis how to perform this one song. When he decided it was too much work, he offered money to the piano teacher to perform while he sang. The guy agreed.

About ten minutes before Victor was going to start his set, the owner walked on the stage and made an announcement.

"Before we welcome Victor Grubb back on stage, one of our regulars wanted to make their debut with us. So please give some encouragement to Ellis Penrose!"

Victor froze mid-sip. Ellis walked on stage with all the confidence of someone who had no idea what they were doing, the piano teacher in tow. As Ellis stepped to the microphone, he said, "I, uh... I wrote this song for someone really special. She's in the crowd tonight. You know who you are."

Lena blushed. Victor and Melanie stopped as they each heard the beginning of a familiar song.

"You son of a bitch," Victor muttered.

Victor saw Melanie whisper something to Lena. She shook her head while Melanie got up from her table and made a beeline for Victor. Victor had written that for her a month into their relationship. She'd always been disappointed that he never recorded it.

"Did you give that to him?" she asked, low and sharp.

Victor shook his head slowly. "I let him read it."

Melanie stood. "He told Lena he wrote this for her."

"Well, he didn't," was all Victor could say.

And just like that, she was across the room. When the song was over, the crowd applauded loudly. Before Victor had any time to react, he was announced back on stage. Victor stood, blinking, still holding his glass. The applause was fading, and Ellis gave him a thumbs-up from the stage like they were old pals sharing a moment.

Victor walked slowly back toward the piano, like a man heading to his own arraignment. The club owner gave him a friendly pat on the back as he passed. It felt like a slap.

He sat at the keys. He glanced toward the back corner where Melanie and Lena sat. Lena looked embarrassed. Melanie looked like a kettle about to shriek.

Victor cracked his knuckles. He didn't say anything. Didn't greet the crowd. Just launched into the opening bars of something moody and wordless— an old Bill Evans tune he could play in his sleep, but tonight it hit differently. Each note dropped like a slow insult. The next two hours felt like a blur for Victor. When he was done, he noticed Ellis was nowhere to be found. Neither was Lena. Todd and Melanie were still there. And Melanie was shooting a stare at him that he hadn't seen in almost two decades.

Victor headed straight for the bathroom, locking the door and taking in everything that had happened. When he was ready to talk with Melanie, he exited the bathroom, but both she and Todd were gone.

Victor sat at the bar, alone. The bartender, Joan came up to him with a beer.

"You alright, Vic?"

"Yeah," said Victor, his eyes given a thousand-yard stare.

"Heard there was some drama tonight."

"Something like that."

"Lena's kinda pissed at Ellis," said Joan.

"What for?" asked Victor, curious.

"I was hearing he lied to her about something."

"Huh," replied Victor. Victor finished his drink and began to make up for the night. When he left the club, he could hear someone screaming. He turned and saw it was Ellis on his phone.

"She's fucking lying!" Ellis exclaimed. "I swear she's fucking lying! … I don't know! I don't know what she fucking does. Just talk to me! I love you! Hello? Hello?! Don't fucking hang up on me!"

Just then, Ellis spotted Victor out of the corner of his eye and stormed up to him.

"Why'd you have to out me like that?!" Ellis yelled.

"Why the hell did you steal my song?!" Victor snapped back.

"I didn't steal anything!"

"Really? What do you call taking something that doesn't belong to you and passing it off as your own?"

"Honestly?" said Ellis. "A business deal."

"You think that money you gave me means you own my songs?"

"What did you think I was paying you for?"

"Last I recall, it was to learn how to play and learn how to write songs."

"Like I would pay you that much for that when you can't even play that well!" Ellis exclaimed. "Why didn't you tell me you wrote that for your ex-wife."

"Because it shouldn't matter because you shouldn't steal anyone's art ever," said Victor. "It's a pretty simple concept. Or is that also something too high brow for you to understand?"

Ellis stepped in, close enough that Victor flinched slightly.

"You should have lied for me!" Ellis demanded.

"Kid," Victor said, calm as a storm gathering offshore, "I've lied for worse people than you."

Then, more quietly: "You don't get to steal something sacred and call it yours just because you need it more. That's not how music works. And you don't lie to someone you have feelings for to make them love you. That's not how that works either."

Ellis looked like he wanted to punch something, but all he could do was shake his head, then walk off muttering, "Fuck this."

Victor stood alone under the soft yellow streetlight. He'd talk to Melanie soon, but not tonight, sort everything out.

He reached into his coat pocket and pulled out a folded napkin—the first scribbled lines of a song written in a younger life. The love that sparked it had vanished, but the truth in the words still held and made him smile, remembering the better times a romance long gone. Love can fade, but it always needs the truth to stand a chance.

ORGAN LESSONS AND THE NEWPORT PHANTOMFIGHTERS

CARINA WAHLSTROM

"SOMETIMES THE ORGAN plays by itself." The maintenance man jingles his keys and slumps in one of the choir pews half awake. A gag reel blares from his phone. "It do that sometimes."

I scan the balcony with the thermal imaging camera. A few hymnals are stacked in the corner, a candelabra stands near the bench, and a ceramic set of figurines depicting the Last Supper sits on a table near the stairs. I expect to find nothing, no white or light blue hints on the TIC that indicate a spirit, and the only discolored blobs are my partner and the janitor's red hot figures. 1 am, third false alarm at Trinity Church this week, let's go.

"Nothing showing," I radio the captain. "You can silence the alarm." Can we go to the hostile possession on Bull Street now?

"Look inside the organ. The swell box. Check the blower room."

If there was anything here, I would have sensed it by now. My ability is better than any of the specter detectors we carry. I don't have to depend on them, and I certainly don't have to depend on Cap.

My partner grabs the TIC and waves it at the organ from top to bottom. Nothing registers. He leans his pike pole against the wall, opens a door to a closet that leads inside the instrument, and vanishes.

I have no idea where he went. I've never been this close to an organ before. Three keyboards plus one on the ground, maybe a dozen pipes. Knobs checker the sides of the keyboards with labels like flute, oboe, clarinet, violin, and choir. Makes no sense to me. I imagine an entire orchestra inside of the instrument somehow connected to these levers, and I'm amazed something like this was invented before the tin can.

Rather than decipher the contraption, I turn to the bench and open it, a simple enough task for a poor boy from Atlanta without any musical ability. Inside the bench is a book of names.

Est. A. D. 1733

Charles Theodore Pachelbel

Berkenhead

Oliver Shaw

Lowell Mason

I flip through pages of signatures and assume at least a hundred people are in the book. Nothing—rather no one—speaks to me, so I toss it back and close the bench.

I flip my radio to TAC-One to eavesdrop on Unit Five while inspecting the keyboards more thoroughly.

"Don't let it get behind you!"

"RIT...Alpha, we need a fishnet!"

"Bravo...Command, status on the entrapment...where's the girl?"

Agh!

A camera flash makes me jump, and I palm-plant the bottom keyboard, my other hand guarding my face from the big, scary source of light.

"Brother, y'all is the baddest things in here. You know that, right? A black man in a white hood."

The glorified custodian smirks at his photo of me donned in my powered air purifying respirator.

"This really is the night shift, eh? Bet your Cap is white. College educated. Only been here half as long as you."

He's two for three.

"Go see for yourself," I say. "Wait downstairs."

He shouldn't be up here anyways without respiratory protection. Senses are useless in detection for most phantomfighters, but the elixirs we use to attract, trap, and expel spirits can liquefy a human from the inside out. I have yet to meet someone else who's able to interact with lost souls prior to possession like I can.

"Does this thing even work?" I punch the keys again with my gloved hand, hitting two or three at a time, only generating rubbery thumps.

"It's not on," he mutters. "Gotta start the blower then pull the drawknob."

What in the world? If ghosts haven't figured out how to start a car, they ain't gonna take the time to find the "on" switch to an oversized piano.

"Joe," my partner calls. He steps out from the closet with all the pipes and grabs the pike pole like a hiking stick. "We need him."

"Why?"

"To access the blower room. We have to go to the cellar."

"MMMM....MMM." Our tour guide stops in the kitchen, two steps shy of what appears to be the cellar door. "Ladies' Bible study night. I smell garlic chicken and buttery dinner rolls." He peaks his head in the fridge. "Oh Lawdy, I'm right!"

"Are you high?" I say.

"You want some?" The refrigerator illuminates his bloodshot eyes. "Banana pudding."

"Leave it out and we may catch the ghost," Richie teases. "Surely they would rather chow on Grandma's chicken parmigiana than the crap in our cans." He's not actually rich, but Richie's been able to afford three engagement rings and is still technically single, so he doesn't fight the nickname. "Maybe you can get the hundred-year-old secret ingredient for the marinara, Joe."

I let the jab go, knowing I'm still earning his trust. As for Sweet Tooth, I push the refrigerator closed and shine my flashlight to the next door. "Cellar. Blower. Organ."

He licks his finger clean. *Pop.* "I was wrong. Lemon." I could've told him that; someone had labeled the container with masking tape. His lips form a puckered grin as he inserts a key into the doorknob and leads us downstairs.

Richie is the only phantomfighter I've met on a tour who I would consider a friend. Black Gumbie reminds me too much of home, but Richie and I bonded over our mutual dislike for Cap after I was hired. He should've been promoted, but the board elected the white guy with a Bachelor of Science in Finance for his "qualifications." We all know it was for "personal reasons."

Though Richie is unsure of me, never giving too much of himself away in conversations because of my sixth sense, I haven't forgotten how he helped me my first week. The other guys on the crew wanted to haze me with prank calls, pretending to be my dead grandfather, but Richie wouldn't let them. I know he understands the pain of losing someone.

"How'd you know to look down here?" I ask, following him down termite-infested, wooden steps without a handlebar. Though he sounds the stairs in front of him with the pole, I'm expecting to fall through any second.

"I'm a volunteer tour guide for the city. On a normal day, I would just talk about the history of the organ, not inspect it. Did you know this was the first church organ shipped from Europe to America? It was commissioned as a gift in 1733 and assembled by Charles Theodore Pachelbel. Though it has a mix of pipes and electrical components, it's still in the original oak case."

"Pachelbel?" I ask, remembering the book of names. "The same Pachelbel as the wedding song?"

"No. Same nationality, different centuries."

He's walking in front of me, but I nod anyway, as if I should've known this.

"Giving tours drew me to this line of work," Richie explains. I had thought it was because his first fiancée had died, but I don't bring it up. "Talking about dead people every weekend made me realize they have unfinished business."

"But you've never spoken to one?"

His hood crinkles, and I assume he's shaking his head. I was in line for a captain's position in Atlanta, especially since I was the only one with the "gift," but my partner who was also in the running saw me smoking a joint after a shift. He blew it out of proportion and told everyone I was getting high on the job and was even dealing out of the station. He received the promotion, and I moved on. Hunting spirits is all that has ever mattered to me once I realized I possessed the "gift."

My grandfather's passing is my earliest memory. Not just because we were close but because he told me a story from his hospital bed that was unforgettable. He warned me Grandma Ida might get a little strange. She may hoard his stuff, continue to buy Romeo y Julieta cigars, and use his glasses to read as if he'd never left.

It all came true. I never wanted to be alone with Grandma Ida. I hated being alone in general, but once I realized I could connect with the other world, I learned how to handle it, how to handle them.

The conversation with my grandfather creeped me out, not because it turned out to be real but because Grandpa told me after he had flatlined.

"Is this it?" I ask, finally at the bottom of the stairs.

"Yeah." Richie inspects the air compressors for paranormal clues and observes the room with the TIC, but the only evidence of another presence is spiderwebs and mouse droppings. "The turbines send constant air to the organ so the player doesn't have to pump with his feet or have someone crank an air pump. One bellow for each manual, and one for the pedalboard."

"These could power a jet plane. Aren't they a little overkill?"

"For one thousand pipes, these work overtime." My jaw drops. "Yeah, they're in the wings, and some are short so you can't see them from the bench." he says.

"You must have been one hell of a tour guide." I wish I would've worked with Richie the first night we responded to an alarm here. He can make a run interesting.

"Aw. You're cute when you're surprised, Joe. You should let me set you up."

The night janitor squeals and slaps his legs. "You make a fine date…if she blind and deaf!"

"Blower room is clear," I radio Cap, ignoring the insult. "We're leaving."

"So that's why you into all this spirit worship," the janitor continues. "They your only friends." He licks his finger again and chuckles as he makes his way upstairs, using the flashlight on his phone to light the way. Richie sprays spirit repellent around the motors and follows, sounding the stairs as he ascends.

"You're not alone."

What was that? That's not Cap's voice. I check my radio to make sure I flipped it back from TAC-One, and it's on our channel.

My flashlight won't turn on, but I spin in the room as if signaling a motion sensor light. My breath fogs the inside of my PAPR, and I shiver. I feel like I took a dive in the Newport Harbor and am standing in my drawers on the coast. I can't find the stairs. I can't even see my hand in front of my face. My radio buzzes, and it speaks to me again.

"Find me."

My body reacts before I know where I'm going. The blowers roar on, and I scatter. I hit wood with my boot, and it splinters and cracks under me. On all fours, climbing the stairs like a gorilla, I race to the light.

RICHIE AND HIS NEW BUDDY, our valiant key holder, don't even look up. I imagine my ear drums are obliterated to powder, but I can still register their smacking on bread the size of softballs. Steam rises off of the buns, and they're dishing out butterflied, parmesan crusted chicken breasts to toss in the microwave next.

"Hey!" I yell. "Did you hear that!"

They stare, mouths half open.

"Thought you were taking a piss," Richie mumbles.

"There's a ghost down there!"

"Quit yelling, man. Eat something." The kitchen whisperer throws a roll at me, but I let it bounce off of my suit.

"Wrap it up." Cap orders over the radio. *"They need us on Bull Street. The neighbor is showing signs of possession. Could take the whole block by sunrise."*

"We're going upstairs," I radio. "We woke something up, and it's ready to play."

I grab Richie and the pike pole, he throws his hood on and grabs the TIC, and Third Wheel grabs the rolls.

"Calm down, Joe," my partner chides. "It's a maintenance cycle."

I choose my words carefully. I had thought the "gift" would be well-accepted among phantomfighters, but they're as resistant to believe one can talk to naked spirits as the general public is to believe in ghosts at all.

"There is something down there our meters can't detect."

"And that only you can hear," he says, blowing me off and muttering something about the psych exam.

"Excuse me?"

"I don't care if you can pass a drug exam, man. But when you hear something no one else can, that's not a gift. That's crazy."

Our shadow, with lemon pudding smeared over his cheek, says the only reason he works here is because they didn't make him pee in a cup. Talks about ghosts with his kids more than God.

What did he say? He has kids!

"I'm not saying you have to believe me. Let's just make sure there won't be another false alarm anytime soon."

"Whatever," Richie says.

"You have kids, don't you?" I ask. Richie grunts. "Do you talk about the afterlife with them?"

"Never! Won't even drive past a graveyard with them."

We're here. I swear the organ buzzes. I look at my radio for instructions, as if I can summon the spirit on cue, unsure of who or what I'm supposed to find. I approach the keys.

I pick the middle manual, and I brace myself for whatever shriek or screech is about to blast through one thousand pipes. Recalling my six months of piano lessons twenty years ago, I push what I think is middle C.

"Black Velvet! Get over here." Nothing came out. "You can't just tell me this thing ain't on. Where the music at?"

"Careful, Brother," the drugged up night workman says smugly. "You startin' to sound like you from around here." He flips a switch, pulls one of the draw knobs, and presses a key.

A howling drone fills the sanctuary. I forget how to breathe. I wish I would've taken a piss in the cellar because I almost wet myself. The last time my heart stopped like this, Prince was on stage playing his guitar solo to "Let's Go Crazy."

Richie points the TIC at the organ, and an icy blue mass lights up the screen, licking out of the pipes. "It's just the compressed air," he says, but his voice cracks. The cloud flickers like thousands of pilot lights, and the colors on the TIC transform to a pulsing hue some-where between blue and white that I've never seen before. He looks side-to-side, and we're half-way surrounded by the unnaturally chilly current.

"Bro, stop. Stop!"

"I ain't touchin' nothin'!"

We look over, and our help is ten feet behind us shooting a video with his phone. His screen would show the outlines of two uniformed men trembling and gawking at an organ that sounds like a train, one armed with a digital club and the other armed with a spear with a curved head. But the screen on the TIC now shows a body shape, oversized, hunched, and running towards us.

We jump back, and Richie sprays a line of spirit repellant between us and the organ. He radios Cap, "Mayday, mayday, mayday!"

The keys on all of the manuals bounce at random. The draw knobs on the sides of the organ pop in and out, and the overhead shutters flap as if in a tornado. The noise is more disorienting than the darkness, and the sound crashes and ricochets around us. Something breaks behind me. One of the disciples from the ceramic Last Supper has fallen to the ground.

A rumbling moan transmits through the radio.

"Help me...find me."

"I found you!" I scream. "What do you want!"

"What's with the yelling again?" Richie hollers, still trying to radio Cap.

My eyes fall on the bench, and I pull it towards me with the pike pole. The organ rapidly repeats the same three descending chords, *Dun...Dun...Dunnn.*

"Black Beauty! Get over here and read these names." I shove the book from the bench to our cameraman, knocking his phone out of his hands. I look for anything else, a secret compartment, a scribble on the wood, a key. "Out loud!" I shout. I glance at the TIC; the figure is blocked by the defensive line of repellent Richie sprayed. It gropes at the invisible line, trying to possess us.

I whip my head around wondering how my directions were unclear, and he's holding the book in one hand and his phone in the other.

"What are you doing?!" I scold. "Seriously? You're texting right now?"

"I gotta use my phone," he says. "I can't read."

I slam the lid to the bench, and Richie grabs the book. He reads. "Charles Theodore Pachelbel. Berkenhead. Oliver-"

The keys lift at once, the knobs return to their resting position, and the wave of ancient, whining wind ceases.

I can hear myself think again, and all three of us lean on each other looking around as if we would find where the sound disappeared to.

"Berkenhead," Richie says, and the radio wails again, *"help me."*

"This must be him. There's no first name."

"So?" I question.

"People listed without a first name, with only the family name, were stillborns," Richie explains. "As a tour guide, I would point these out when passing cemeteries."

"So we need to write his first name?"

He shrugs uncertainly. "Worth a shot. Maybe he can't move on if the universe thinks he was never born."

"This is a church," I argue. "Wouldn't God know who he is and when he died?"

No one has an answer. We can't explain anything that's happened tonight. Why question God now?

"Well, how are we going to find his name?" I groan, imagining we'll be here another two hours.

"I bet it was John," our illiterate friend pipes up.

I roll my eyes. "And how do you know?"

He points to the Last Supper, and to the broken figurine on the floor. "John's the disciple that fell."

Richie and I gape, and a mixture of annoyance and relief surges through my arteries. I want this night to be over. I fumble for a pen, and toss it to Richie. "Try it."

His hand shakes. Mine would too, tampering with a three hundred-year-old document without certainty it would do any good. He practices looping the letters in the air a few times and taps the pen on the carpet so it doesn't bleed into the book before placing the tip on the page.

Berkenhead, John

Nothing happens. The room remains dark. The organ remains silent. But I let out a breath and my shoulders uncoil one filament at a time. Richie slowly raises the TIC in front of us, and the organ is a solid royal blue.

"Alpha...Cap. What's your status?"

I never thought I could be so glad to hear Cap's voice.

"Disregard mayday. Spirit is pacified. We're coming down."

THE SUN CRESTS over the horizon back at the station. Richie and I have both deconned and doffed our suits, and by the time we shower, our shift is almost over. Willy, the nightguard, gifted us with the rest of the lemon pudding. Normally we would dive in to celebrate a job well done, but neither of us have an appetite. We stand outside behind the truck with steaming cups of black coffee, and the pink, golden halo of light warms my forehead.

Cap said he was trying to find backup for us at the church, but all units were at Bull Street. We would've had to wait for mutual aid from Tiverton. He said we did a good job and should apply for a promotion next round.

"Why did you come here of all places?" Richie asks.

"Block Island," I say. "Less than fifty miles away, right? Maybe the only site in America with more hauntings than Atlanta."

"Remind me next shift, and I can tell you all kinds of stories from that island."

I look over, and he has a mischievous grin on his face. I'm not sure if he's thinking of ghost stories or escapades with one of his fiancées.

"Good place for a romantic getaway?"

"Oh, haha. I suppose so. You've heard the rumors."

"Hey, it's your life, But yeah, I have."

Richie raises his mug to his lips but doesn't take a sip. He can't meet my gaze, but for the first time since I've known him, he looks like he needs a friend.

"It wasn't right what I was doing to those girls."

I don't know what the hell he could mean by that. I tense up and wait for him to finish.

"I loved them. I really did. But I never stopped loving Deborah, the kids' mom. I could only think of her when I was with them."

I relax. I can't relate. No kids, never married, no siblings, parents divorced. Began working in paranormal protection and prevention right after high school and hardly have any friends because of it. All I have is my job.

"Can I tell you a secret?" he asks.

I hesitate. "What is it?"

"I don't know if I thought it'd be romantic or jealous or what, but now the thought makes me sick." Richie pours out his coffee and lets his mug hang from his index finger. "I have no business getting married, Joe. I thought if I got engaged again, Deborah might come back and…possess one of them."

He hangs his head and covers his eyes with his hand. I want to say something reassuring or encouraging, but I'm out of good comebacks. So I place my hand on his shoulder. I can't imagine how many years he's held that in, mourning the woman he loves and raising their kids by himself.

"I'm sorry I give you a hard time for talking to spirits," he says quietly. "I was bitter. I want what you have." I know he's thinking he'd give anything to talk to Deborah again. "You can't—-"

"No," I cut him off. I can't raise the dead or call on them. I'm not a transmitter, only a receiver. "But I would like to hear more about her sometime. Whenever you're ready."

The tones for shift change go off, and we return to the station. The sun has risen, a perfect circle of light resting on the horizon. Our apparatuses shine in the bay reflecting a new day, a fresh start. We hang up our radio straps in our lockers and return the radios to the chargers. Until next time.

"Do you want to come over for breakfast?" he asks, and I nod. "Hey, I think that's the first time I've seen you smile."

I laugh and smile even bigger. "Yeah, I suppose it is."

No matter how many times we decon, no matter how long we stand in the sun, we'll always carry something inside that can't be pruned or untied. We'll carry it until it's ready to make its presence known, manifesting in unnatural, illogical ways.

Richie and I swore an oath to bear a burden for society, to keep the public safe, and just now, we've sworn a silent oath to bear each other's burdens as well, a security of brotherhood.

"I'd love to come over for breakfast."

And man, I love this job.

GRANDMA ERDA'S PIANO

JAY HELTZER

For Yıldız Dağdelen who never said "no," and Bruno Ast who often said "yes."

I WAS AFRAID of my grandmother, but only as Erda, the Earth Goddess, emerging from a forest green mist with white eyes staring at me like celestial search lights. Her debut at the 1964 Bayreuth Festival lived on a poster in her living room, celebrating a singular moment of her long operatic life, which otherwise frightened me as a child.

"Who's that?" I remember asking my mother, pointing at the image.

"That's Grandma Katherine as Erda."

I used to think her first name was "Grandma," and her last name was "Kathrine," pronounced like "marine" with a T added before the R. The moment I saw a piece of mail addressed to Mrs. Kathrine Walzman, the same last name as mine and my mother's, I understood that not everything was as it seemed compared to first impressions. She was always my loving grandmother, but I could never shake the poster's image from my mind. How could the same charming old woman with the deep voice who called me "Little Darling," while sneaking candies into my hand out of my mother's view, be the Norse god emerging from green-shadowed clouds with a judgmental glare from a poster hanging in the center of her living room wall?

A massive grand piano created a safety barrier between me and the frightening image. As much as I appreciated its defensive blockade, Erda's stark white eyes always found me across the delta. A 1960s pop art warning of the impending end of the gods, as well as a reminder not to touch grandma's beloved musical instrument.

My grandmother had a face that could tell a thousand tales, express a thousand emotions, and a voice so deep and resonant, I wondered if it came from the same brown velvet lining of her couch. Her mellifluous words could warm a room and make winter's chill irrelevant. She expressed adoration for her family, but the framed poster of her haunting shadowed face was unavoidably the foundational view of my grandmother, the Earth Goddess.

It wasn't only menacing stares in the short span of time I shared with Grandma Katherine. There were plenty of casual memories like my mother and her seated in the living room in red barrel chairs talking about things her doctor said, or about Gladys the nosy neighbor, or stories like how her late husband, Grandpa Yosef, whom I never knew, could prepare a wild turkey caught from a hunt, leaving at least one buckshot pellet in the carcass for "good luck." Although he was a skilled craftsman in the woodshop, creating cabinets and furniture for many decades, she was the primary source of their fantastic life together.

After an average career of supporting and chorus roles across Europe's not-as-impressive stages, conductor Berislav Klobučar's invitation to perform at the legendary opera house solidified her place in history. While Erda only appears in two scenes among the four operas of Wagner's massive journey known as "Der Ring des Nibelungen," Grandma Katherine's performance made her a star on the stage, and thus, a postered idol within her home.

The wall surrounding the verdant tribute was a collection of smaller black and white and color-faded photos showcasing her joyous memories. Laughing alongside tuxedoed men carrying musical scores and batons, dressed in dirty rags with haggard makeup in other opera roles, and on vacation with Grandpa Yosef and my mother as a child, on a boat on a lake in the sun, all of them young and carefree. Photographic stories of a happy woman who lived a meaningful and rewarding life. I always believed Grandma's genuine words of praise and love. However, my young imagination added Erda's unspoken threat of "...or else," commanding an unyielding appreciation of Grandma Katherine, similar to warning Wotan of the impending end of the gods. It produced complicated feelings of love and fear for a five-year-old to process.

Drawing my eyes away from the poster, they often fell on her grand piano, lighting my curiosity as it caught midday sunlight. Its ebony body transferred beams of resonant energy through the room like a vibrant chord sustaining forever. To a young child, a piano of any design offers eighty-eight possibilities, with three mysterious magic foot pedals which add color to the already kaleidoscopic tones. Some of my friends had upright pianos in their houses. Unlike my grandmother's pristine instrument, they housed random books, magazines, and picture frames on top of the lid. Often, they had a familiar water stain on the lid from a cool glass or an overflowing planter. Their pianos produced repetitive scales and quaint childlike melodies about mulberry bushes and farmers who work in dells. To my friends, it was a torture device. In my grandmother's home, it was a beacon of opportunity.

I remember the keyboard's lure, summoning me like a piper's infectious melody, beckoning me to follow. A horizon of white keys lay before me, each one offering a different tonal color. Pairs and trios of black keys lay in between, adding to the mystery. I understood the numeric pattern of their arrangement, but I was unable to crack the harmonic code hiding beneath the surface.

One lazy afternoon during a visit, the compulsion to experience the magic of the instrument was too strong to ignore. After a hesitant approach to the piano, my right index finger gently pressed one of the white keys in the middle, producing a pleasant soft tone like a keyhole peek into heaven. I looked over to the furthest right, repeating the same action on the uppermost note, and a high-pitched *ping* emerged, like a woodland creature asking for discovery. Looking to the left, the lowest note sounded deep and mysterious, like a dark bottomless cave groaning. If a soft touch sounded quiet, I wondered, then hoped loud touches would be louder. My finger found its bravery, applying more strength and creating a more euphoric sound. If single notes asked simple questions, groups of notes asked questions requiring more information, or perhaps, providing answers. If several adjacent keys together made a crunch, then skipping every other note at once made a delightful sound, and a combination of the two created a most magnificent discordant noise. My ears rang with joy as I accelerated through a sonic journey. Up, down, chords, improvised melodies, my fingers traveled far and wide as fast and as excited as they could move. Only five years old, and I was the maker of magic. With every articulation, I yearned for more as my fingers extended into wide platforms, capturing as many notes as possible, filling the air with such amazing and harmonious joy…

Until she said, "No!"

I had no awareness of my grandmother's location before I began playing, forgetting the world existed as I explored. She reminded me of her presence with a forceful and demanding shout. Her expressive face now said rage. I was frightened. I vowed never to touch the piano again, but I only heard it in my head. I had disturbed the gods. Erda was upset.

On the next visit, a month later, I saw the piano in a different light. It held the same appeal, but I remained cautious enough to not touch it, revering it like an art museum installation. I found other things to do and occupy my mind, yet the behemoth was always there, watched over by Erda. There was no way I would tempt the gods a second time.

I remember sneaking through the pantry searching for a midday snack. Instead of finding a cereal box with bright colors and cute animated characters, all I unearthed were blurry pictures of creamed oats or milk-coated brown sticks drifting in a bowl.

An ominous sound emerged from the living room, pulling me away from my mission. A terrifying harmonic premonition of bad things to come. Deep, thick chords that warned of curses, raised caution for trespassers, and fomented doom to those not heeding its threats. Despite the foreboding musical messages, I tiptoed from the kitchen, peeking around the corner into the living room. My grandmother sat hunched over the keyboard, with her back curved like bent steel, as she cast spells two, four, seven, eight notes at a time. What she was playing must have been crafted by winged warlocks and dark-minded mages who practiced an illicit craft. I was cautious not to make a single sound, so as not to disturb the monsters summoned by my grandmother at the keys.

There was no sheet music on the piano, so she was either playing from memory or crafting a musical elixir on the fly. I was mesmerized and remained stock-still, not blinking, wondering if demons would emerge from the piano's raised lid like bats streaming from an underground cave. The sounds matched Erda's expression on the wall and I expected her to come to life and chastise me for disturbing the moment. The final chord faded and sat in the air like an ornate chandelier swinging on a single thread, ready to fall to the ground, bringing more tension than relief. What was that hypnotic piece she conjured up?

Like a lightning bolt striking in a storm, my grandmother turned on the bench and stared at me with the same expression as Erda's look of warning from the poster. Her head tilted back at a slight angle, her mouth agape in horrid disbelief, and her eyes open wide, as if Erda herself predicted my own doom. Although the moment felt like an eternity of judgment and fear, it lasted a mere second before I turned and ran to where my mother sat reading outside. I wanted to scream with anguish, but again, the sound resonated solely in my head, never emerging from my mouth. As I opened the sliding door, I heard my grandmother's deep cackling laughter, shouting for me to return.

"Come back, little darling," as if she still wished to predict my doom.

"What's wrong?" asked my mother as I crawled into her lap, bypassing the book in her hands. I didn't want to answer. I didn't have to answer. I was safe in my mother's arms from Erda and her music, that is, until my grandmother joined us outside. "Not a fan of Rachmaninov, I guess," she said with a throaty laugh.

Hours later, after dinner at her favorite Italian restaurant, I held onto my lingering remorse. Twice I had incurred the wrath of Erda, thinking I violated a sacred space or broken an unwritten rule. I didn't know her jump scare was solely for her amusement. As we said goodbye, there was no mention of it at all. She once again called me "Little Darling" and kissed my head before my mother carried me to the car. As we drove off, Grandma waved, but all I could do was stare back from my side window, afraid to anger her any more than I already had.

Two weeks later, wails of pain from my mother's side of a phone call stopped me in my tracks. I had never heard such agony before. After hanging up, she came to me in the playroom and told me that Grandma Kathrine passed away while out with friends. Something about her brain getting sick. My mother was sharing painful words with me, but all I heard in my young mind were her cries from the phone call moments before. I vividly remember staring into her reddened, puffy eyes while she spoke, saying words I didn't understand. Something bad happened to Grandma's head, not Erda, the Earth Mother, destroyed from within by loud piano sounds, or the twilight of the gods wreaking havoc in their realm. But, in my young, curious, and frightened mind, it could have been.

PHONE CALLS with mom never quite convey the emotions behind my tone of voice. Either that or I haven't learned how to say "No" to her.

"She'd want you to have it."

"She didn't know me past five years old, Mom. How do you know what she'd want for me?"

Grandma Katherine's piano was on its way to me from my mother's house, where it had lived for the last thirty years. It remained unused, minus my daughter, Ella, showing off what she learned in school lessons. Residing in my small house, it will gain a modicum of use, making an argument against its arrival that much more difficult.

"The instrument has quite a legacy behind it. Did you know that Sir Georg Solti played it during a rehearsal with Grandma Kathrine? That was one of the pictures on her wall."

I somewhat remember the image of a smiling bald man sitting at a piano, conducting my grandmother.

She stood next to it, singing. Her mouth was so round mid-note, I thought she was navigating a bite of scalding mashed potato. My once-young imagination continued to have fun with Grandma Katherine's memories, even as an adult.

"Ella can take her lessons on it," Mom continued. "Your grandmother would love to know it is getting good use. Besides, the apartment I am moving to doesn't have room for it. I know she'd want it to stay in the family and not let some vagrants abuse it."

The image of the poor, starving artists from *La Boheme* sullying a grand piano came to mind. I opted not to argue using this point as well.

The following week, two husky and hirsute piano movers negotiated the enormous ebony beast into my home. Once reassembled, it filled the void where my ex's favorite couch once occupied our shared space and time. As the larger of the two men collected their tools and equipment, the other flipped through the paperwork to gain my signature. Before handing it over with a greasy ballpoint pen clipped to the top of the pages, he said to his partner, "These are two of three. What's missing?" His partner said, "There's a flat parcel, too. I'm getting it. Stop nagging."

The piano lid stood open, eager for sound. With the black padded bench seated in front of the keys, I couldn't imagine what was missing. A tall rectangle wrapped in a dirty, grey moving blanket entered my home, like an old geometric horse entering a new stable.

My fears returned with the reveal beneath the blanket of the green, harrowing face of my childhood staring at me once again. Erda, the Earth Goddess, the foundation of my grandmother's memory and the source of my pre-adolescent nightmares, had entered the sanctuary of my living room, uninvited and with no intention of leaving.

The mover leaned it up against the wall, in its likely place of honor beyond the piano, as it once hung in my grandmother's home. I hadn't laid eyes on the familiar tormenting face since the last time I saw my grandmother alive.

"You sent the *Siegfried* poster, too?" I asked my mom in a text.

"I thought you loved it," she replied. Maybe she's thinking of a different child from a family I never knew. Unsure whether to thank her or complain, I pocketed my phone before incurring Erda's wrath via emojis.

Thirty years later, my adult brain wrestled against my childhood memories as the green goddess continued her gaze upon me. My fear was now tempered and reserved, despite the conditioning of trauma. Was it because I knew better, or because this was the first time my sightline was higher than Erda's? Temporarily anchored to the floor instead of the wall, she was glaring at my kneecaps, and not down at me from eight feet above.

An hour later, Ella walked in from school, smiling at the sight of the delivery. She went directly to the keyboard and began playing her most recent polonaise, but paused mid-phrase, noticing the green lady propped up behind the piano and leaning against the wall. The hesitation and uncertainty on her face were likely the same as mine when I was less than half her age upon first acknowledgement of the image. Perhaps we shared the same concerns, a generation apart.

"What's that?" she asked with teenage skepticism.

"That's your great-grandmother."

"What's she doing, and what's a Siegfried?"

Recalling my fears, Ella's hardened curiosity threw me off my game.

"Remember, I told you my grandmother was an opera singer? That is her as Erda, the Earth Mother, from Norse mythology. It was her biggest role. The opera, *Siegfried,* was the highlight of her career."

Knowing Ella's quick tendency to dismiss the value of something if it doesn't benefit her important existence, I waited for her to move on to something more crucial on her phone. Instead, she stared, she contemplated. Then, she grinned.

"My great-grandmother was a Norse opera goddess? Cool. Can we hang that near the piano?"

"Sure thing, little darling."

Tremolo

John William McMullen

THE BLEACHERS BUZZED with gossip, but Matilda McGuinn barely noticed. Her eyes drifted to the folded flyer in her purse announcing that evening's all-Mozart concert—*An Evening with Mozart,* featuring a dazzling virtuoso performing the *Piano Concerto No. 24*, with the *Requiem Mass* as the finale.

She could almost hear the crisp notes of the piano, the dark swell of strings, and a heavenly chorus; the slow ascent of sound above the ballfield, melodies blending with the chatter of the children. For a moment she was elsewhere—far from the dust and babble, floating in the sonorous concert hall where everything shimmered and all was well with the world.

A sharp crack of a bat, followed by a foul ball whizzing past her head, jolted Matilda back to the little-league diamond. The imagined orchestra vanished, jarringly replaced with sour notes of irritation and off-key noise of reality.

"River. That good-for-nothing River! How did Megan let that fool worm his way into her life?" Matilda snarled.

Next to her sat Esther Schneider. Their grandchildren played on the same team in the summer-fall league, and the two women had become fast friends—drawn together less by the game than by their shared grievances: their mutual dismay and commiseration over their daughters' terrible tastes in men and lovers.

"Bless your heart," Esther shook her head.

"I can't believe both of our daughters have borne the children of losers," Matilda muttered, still fuming.

"Don't remind me," Esther sighed. "I've told Lisa to get rid of her loser."

Matilda poked a finger into Esther's shoulder. "That damned muddle-headed preacher at *The Church of the Tabernacle of Holiness, Salvation, Grace & More* up and married my daughter, Megan, to that idiot freeloader, River."

"Pitiful liberal preacher," Esther shook her head. "My daughter's lame-brained, poor excuse for a man, Cain Pole, got fired from his job. He went in to work higher than a kite. *Cain Pole.* I mean, what kind of idiot mother names her kid Cain if his last name's going to be Pole? And in the Bible, didn't Cain kill Abel? Well, I just wish none of it had ever happened. Why the hell do good girls get mixed up with such bums?"

"I don't know," Matilda said, "but sometimes I pray I'll wake up one morning and hear the wonderful news that River is history."

"Oh, me too, girl," Esther nodded eagerly. "At least my Lisa isn't married to Cain. That way—if and when it happens—it'll be easier to be rid of him."

Just then, one of the kids smacked the ball. Parents and grandparents cheered and clapped as the little ones ran the bases.

"Good morning, ladies," a young blond man called out, stepping down from a few rows behind them. "Sounds like you could use some help."

Matilda turned and found herself staring at his winsome face. "Excuse me?"

"Oh, hi. I'm Gus. Gus Vidar." He extended his hand to each of them, shaking warmly. His tousled sandy hair nearly hid his eyes, and his St. Louis Cardinals shirt, shredded jeans, and leather sandals gave him a rugged, easy charm.

"Nice to meet you, Gus," Esther said, caught off guard by his virile presence.

"Sorry to intrude," he continued, lowering his voice. "I couldn't help overhearing your conversation about your daughters. Those two guys sound like scum."

"They are," Matilda harrumphed, rolling her eyes. "But what can you do?"

"Plenty." Gus paused, glancing around before sliding down another row to sit behind them.

"What?" Matilda asked, watching him move closer.

"Well," he leaned in, "let's just say your prayers have been answered."

"*What?*" she repeated, uneasily.

"Shush, let the boy speak," Esther chided Matilda.

Gus rubbed his palms together, scanning the bleachers as if ensuring privacy. "What if your daughter's idiot husband never came home one day? Would you miss him?"

"Certainly not," Matilda said, twisting her mouth.

"Well, then," Gus said softly. "One down, one to go."

"Excuse me?" Matilda asked.

"Yes. Poof. Gone. He disappears. Forever. Painless. And cheap."

"What?" Both women recoiled.

"Relax," Gus smiled. "I won't charge much."

"*Charge?!*" Matilda's eyes widened as her voice cracked.

Esther clutched her purse, shrinking into herself.

"Sir, I don't think that's funny at all!" Matilda snapped. "I may not like my son-in-law, but I wouldn't kill him."

"Exactly," Gus smiled and tilted his head. "You wouldn't have to. That's where I come in."

"Oh, no, you don't," Esther said, shifting closer to Matilda, away from him.

"Don't worry," Gus continued. "I can take care of them both for you. It might take me a day or two, but I'll get it done." The man's tone changed—light, almost playful.

"You're not right, young man." Matilda's face hardened. "This is illegal. I'll call the police!"

"Call the *police*? On *whom*?" Gus asked, smiling faintly. "You're the one who said you wouldn't miss him. *River*, wasn't it?"

"Matilda," Esther whispered sharply. "Don't answer him. Don't say anything!"

Gus turned to her. "And your daughter's man is Cain Pole."

"He is *not* my son-in-law," Esther snapped, "and I certainly won't give you the man's name."

"But that *is* his name," Gus smiled slowly. "Isn't it?"

Esther's silence was answer enough.

"Matilda, let's move," she said suddenly, rising to her feet.

They grabbed their purses and hurried to the far side of the bleachers.

Moments later, Esther's grandson stepped up to bat. The crowd clapped and shouted encouragement. When Esther looked back, Gus Vidar was gone.

"Good riddance," Matilda muttered with a laugh.

"But you don't think—" Esther began, her voice faltering.

"Of course not," Matilda said, shaking her head. "He's probably on meth or something."

"Yeah." Esther exhaled, clutching her purse tight. "You're right," she whispered, though the words fell flat.

As the last batter struck out and the umpire called the game, families gathered their folding chairs and the crowd began to thin. The late afternoon sunlight stretched long across the field, turning to gold and shadows while Esther stared at the empty bleachers where Gus had interrupted her world.

Matilda reminded Esther of that evening's symphony concert. "Tonight's pianist is a talented young man," she said. "I saw him on TV this morning—he's been playing since he was four."

"That's nice," Esther replied, forcing a smile as she thought about what dress she might wear. But Gus Vidar's words hauntingly echoed in her mind, faint but unshakable, beneath the melody of her thoughts.

Poof. Gone.

Disappears. Forever.

Painless.

And cheap.

And his quiet promise—*It might take me a day or two, but I'll get it done*—resounded and coiled inside her gut—an unsolvable knot of dread, lodged less in her stomach than in her soul.

EVENING SETTLED OVER the city like a hush before the downbeat as Matilda and Esther made their way to the concert at Covert Symphony Hall. The setting sun gave way to streets glowing with the soft amber of street lamps while the autumn air carried the scent of rain and dying leaves, and, for Esther, it felt like the world itself was holding its breath.

The limestone façade of Symphony Hall glowed in the last violet of dusk as Matilda and Esther made their way up the steps. Inside the marbled lobby, their footsteps echoed upon the stone, as chandeliers floated above the dark varnish and velvet of the hall. They presented their tickets at the entrance and an usher handed them that night's program before guiding them to their seats near the left aisle.

Anticipation rippled through the gathered assemblage as the patrons took their seats. Meanwhile the orchestra members tuned their instruments. Clarinets, oboes, bassoons, flutes, and horns breathed forth; stringed sighs from violins, violas, cellos and thrums from the timpani and the double bass sections collided into a murmur of sound and glinting brass in the stage lights.

Esther's heart was still uneasy from the morning's encounter at the ball diamond, but Matilda seemed to have moved on. "You worry too much," she had said in the car.

Esther opened her program.

Mozart's Music of Mourning and Mercy: Requiem for the Living

Tonight's concert begins in ritual darkness, journeys through storm and solitude, and ends with Mozart's great prayer of release and peace.

Mozart's Masonic Funeral Music (1785), written to honor a fallen brother of his Masonic lodge, evokes the weight of communal grief—its solemn sonorities recalling ancient rituals of remembrance and collective mourning. It is a meditation on death. Though brief, its shared sorrow reminds us that death is never borne alone but held within the embrace of community and the bonds of human love.

The opening chords move with solemn weight—a slow procession of low strings and brass that feels both ancient and dignified. As the music unfolds, gentle woodwinds weave in, their lines rising and falling like human voices offering comfort. The phrases breathe slowly, each one shaped with care, as if Mozart were speaking in tones of grief and hope at once.

Though brief, the piece lingers: a meditation on mortality and brotherhood that leaves the listener in reverent silence.

The audience hushed. The house lights dimmed. Then silence.

From a side entrance, the salt and pepper haired maestro in tails strode to the podium and bowed to the audience amid applause. The conductor quickly turned to the seated musicians and took up his baton.

The first strains of Mozart's *Masonic Funeral Music* ascended from the orchestra. Clarinets spoke in solemn whispers, French horns answered with quiet resonance, and the strings carried the melody upon a wave. The music felt heavier than mere sound— dense, ceremonial, almost breathing with grief.

The incident upon the bleachers still lingered in Esther's mind: Gus's sharp, knowing smile and the way he'd said, *"Poof. Gone."* The memory pulsed beneath the music seemingly in tandem with her heartbeat and breath, each chord a whisper of fear.

As the piece unfolded, the low strings moved with stately weight; the brass glowed like candlelight in a crypt. Gentle woodwinds rose and fell like human voices offering solace and comfort. When the final chord faded, the silence that followed felt reverent, as if the whole hall were praying.

The orchestra concluded the work and there was a breathless pause before those gathered slowly began to applaud. The conductor turned and bowed and exited the stage.

Mildred turned to Esther and smiled. "That was lovely. Sad, but lovely."

Esther nodded. "If you like death."

The house lights brightened. The violin, viola, and cello sections of the orchestra then stood and began moving their music stands and chairs. Three orchestra crew members dressed in black wheeled out an elegant Steinway grand piano and put it in position to the left of center stage while the string sections repositioned themselves on stage.

Esther reached for her program and opened it to read.

Piano Concerto No. 24 in C Minor, K. 491, by Wolfgang Amadeus Mozart.

One of only two concertos he wrote in a minor key, it stands among his darkest and most dramatic works—stormy, restless, and unresolved, a lament of longing and the human struggle against fate. Composed in the spring of 1786 at the height of his powers, it inhabits a world of turbulence and shadow.

The first movement opens with stern orchestral chords that give way to a piano line of restlessness, voices contending in unseen conflict.

The second movement offers a lyrical respite—an aria without words—though the shadows never entirely recede.

In the final movement, Mozart transforms a simple theme into variations. In the fifth variation, he turns to fugal counterpoint building toward a fierce conclusion that leaves not triumph but awe, as though something vital has been both revealed and withheld.

Mozart's Piano Concerto No. 24 in C Minor will be performed by the piano virtuoso Augustus Villano Vidaraski, a native of St. Louis, Missouri.

Below were press notes:

Vidaraski's genius burns with brilliance that borders on madness. Each note is precise, each silence deliberate. His art hovers on the precipice—where mastery becomes obsession, and genius edges toward madness. —— The St. Louis Post-Dispatch

Vidaraski commands the piano with fearless precision and fierce passion, his playing shimmering with beauty—as though the keys remember secrets long forgotten. —— The Washington Post

His virtuosity captivates, drawing the listener into a realm where light and shadow entwine, a tapestry of sound lingering long after the final note fades. —— The Cincinnati Enquirer

The lights dimmed again. Esther looked up from her program. The conductor returned to the podium, and the audience grew still. From the wings, the pianist appeared—tall, ruddy, fair-haired, immaculate in black. He moved with deliberate grace, expression serene, a faint smile upon his lips. Each gesture carried the weight of intention: the bow to the audience, the nod to the maestro, the quiet seating at the grand Steinway.

Applause echoed through the hall, washing over him like surf against stone.

Esther's breath caught. The light brushed his face, and for an instant, the resemblance was uncanny. The same tousled blond hair. The same calm, unsettling smile. But this man wore a tuxedo, not a tattered Cardinals shirt. *Augustus Villano Vidaraski was a piano virtuoso,* the program read.

The conductor raised his baton. Silence gathered. The pianist sat motionless, his hands resting on his lap, seemingly lost in thought and meditation. Then, with a breath, the orchestra began—a haunted phrase in the strings, rising and falling like breath. The woodwinds followed, then the thunder of the full orchestra.

A full two minutes passed before Vidaraski lifted his head. He raised his hands and answered the orchestra—clear, restrained, precise. The dialogue began: piano and orchestra in conversation, tension and release. His fingers traced phrases that shimmered between fury and grace. The movement surged; the piano resisted, then yielded, then rose again in dark banter.

For Esther, the musical tension recalled Gus Vidar's obscene suggestion that Cain and River's deaths would be *Painless. And cheap.* She shifted in her seat and lowered her gaze.

"He's talented, isn't he?" Matilda leaned close, whispering.

"Yes," Esther replied, forcing the words out, her voice taut. "Very."

Matilda leaned back, eyes closed, letting the music wash over her.

Esther tried to do the same, but the melody rang hollow though the pianist's hands moved with fearless precision and grace.

Matilda reached for Esther's hand. "I'm so glad we came."

Esther nodded, though her heart was still perturbed and uneven. The shadow of Gus Vidar lingered, hidden behind the golden glow of Symphony Hall. *It might take me a day or two, but I'll get it done.*

As Esther watched the movement of the pianist's hands, the notes carried some of the fear away, but the calm was short-lived. The stranger's words pulsed beneath the melody, impossible to silence. *Disappears. Forever.* At the end of the first movement, the pianist, Vidaraski, lifted his hands from the keyboard and smiled faintly, as though acknowledging a secret no one else knew.

The second movement began—a fragile adagio, tender as forgiveness; a wordless aria suspended in light.

The adagio gave Esther pause, and she thought of her daughter—of how she loved Cain—and how perhaps she had been too hasty in her judgment of the young man. She glanced at Matilda and wondered if her friend, too, was reconsidering her opinion of Megan's marriage to River.

The third movement began like a storm gathering light. Vidaraski drew the orchestra in as he expounded upon Mozart's fugal variations. The orchestra followed his lead and the music built toward its cadenza, each measure drawing tighter, brighter, faster.

Briefly Esther felt the weight of Gus Vidar's words lifting, carried away by the music.

In the final notes of the variations, Vidaraski's hands commanded each phrase with radiating brilliance throughout the score. The tension climbed—theme and variation, struggle and release—until the piano and orchestra sparkled with a subtle tremolo foreshadowing of its finale.

But just as the music swelled into its fugue—a sharp, metallic snap of a piano string cut the reverent air, slicing across the orchestral strings and arpeggios, tearing through the harmonies like a whip.

The violent, discordant note rang out—abrupt, jarringly contradicting the melody. The dissonant note echoed in the hall above the piano and orchestra, ringing longer than it should have—lingering, deliberate, as if it *wanted* to be heard.

The first violin froze mid-bow. The conductor's baton hovered in midair. Murmurs undulated through the audience.

Vidaraski did not move. His hands were suspended above the keys, eyes fixed forward as if the broken string itself had struck him. Then he lifted his head toward the conductor. A brief nod passed between them.

Vidaraski then dropped his hands upon the keys and slid into the cadenza, each note a careful negotiation, his right hand compensating for the missing key with uncanny precision. Vidaraski's playing grew fiercer, freer—as if the break had released something inside him, reshaping each phrase, transforming the wounded piano into redeemed art. The cadenza was more daring now, imbued with an eerie intensity, haunted by the echo of the broken piano string. The orchestra followed, swept into his momentum.

But for Esther, the cadenza no longer dazzled. A subtle dissonance lingered beneath the melody. Gus Vidar had made his way into Symphony Hall. Esther heard his voice—soft, mocking, certain: *Your prayers have been answered.*

When the final note of the concerto sounded it left amazement in its place. The audience erupted in applause.

The broken string still curled above the open grand piano, quivering in the stage lights like a steel serpent.

Vidaraski stood slowly from the piano, bowed to the conductor, then to the orchestra, and then turned to the audience, his expression triumphant. As the ovation swelled, the orchestra members lowered their instruments. By now the audience was on its feet.

Vidaraski's gaze swept the hall—and found the two women. The corners of his mouth lifted—not in pride, but in recognition. He smiled that same slow, deliberate smile. For the briefest moment, his eyes caught Esther's.

Esther's stomach moiled. The applause continued, but she barely heard it. The broken string still sang, refusing to die away.

Esther looked at Matilda and then at the pianist. His blonde locks of hair pulled back from his face revealed his wry smile. *How could she not have seen it before?*

She retrieved her program and studied the pianist's name: *Augustus Villano Vidaraski*. She then looked up at the pianist, then again at his printed name, examining the letters carefully—*Au**gus**tus Villano **Vidar**aski. Gus Vidar?*

"Isn't he something?" Matilda leaned over, applauding. "Handsome as sin, too," she whispered with a smile.

Esther's mouth was dry. "Matilda," she said, barely moving her lips, "look at him."

"I am looking," Matilda said, still smiling.

"No — *really* look!" Esther implored. "He saw me. He saw *us*!"

"He saw all of us," Matilda whispered back, fumbling with her program. "He's just acknowledging the audience."

But Esther knew better. There was a glint behind his smile — polite, practiced, and terribly knowing.

Esther grimaced. "It's him!"

"Who?"

"Him!" Esther pointed. "The pianist!"

"He's *what?*"

"He's that man—*Gus Vidar*—from the ballpark this morning!"

"Don't be ridiculous," Matilda laughed.

The pianist returned for another bow to the audience.

Matilda's gaze sharpened, her smile fading.

"Look at him!" Esther insisted. "See?"

Matilda looked intently at the young man upon the stage. Her smile drained from her face as she stared at the pianist.

Then Vidaraski turned and looked toward the audience and seemingly caught both Esther and Matilda's eyes. He smiled and bowed.

Upon rising he smiled once more—his slow and deliberate grin—and looked directly at the women, as if acknowledging a secret only they could understand.

"You don't think...." Matilda's eyes grew wide.

"I don't think. I *know*," Esther replied, her voice trembling. "Let me show you!"

She opened her program and pointed to the pianist's full name, *Augustus Villano Vidaraski* showing Matilda the **G-U-S** in Augustus and **V-I-D-A-R** in Vidaraski.

Matilda held her breath and slowly pointed to his middle name: ***Villano***. "That's Italian for ***villain***!"

Neither woman dared speak his name.

Esther folded her program shut and pressed into her purse.

When they looked again toward the stage, Vidaraski had already turned—his back to the audience as he made his way offstage. He quickly returned for another bow to the adoring fans.

Esther still heard the discord echoing in her mind.

The applause thundered on, polite and oblivious, but for Esther and Matilda, the night had turned. Mozart's music had ended—but the echo of that broken string still sang.

Vidaraski returned to the stage and bowed once more before vanishing into the wings of the stage.

As the applause died away, the theater lights brightened for intermission. The assemblage began moving toward the aisles. The air in the hall felt charged, as though from an invisible storm.

Esther and Matilda joined the slow current of people drifting toward the grand lobby foyer. Whispers circled around them—praise for the brilliance of the pianist, fragments of awe and admiration. A small crowd had gathered at the foot of the grand staircase, drawn by something—or someone.

Esther stopped short.

There he was.

Gus Vidar.

He stood by the stairwell with practiced ease. On each arm, he escorted a woman—one, a poised brunette in a long black gown and diamond choker; the other, an older, pale heavyset blonde in a pastel floral dress and designer flats.

Matilda leaned close. "It *is* him!"

Vidaraski looked up at Esther and Matilda. "Good evening, ladies."

"Good evening," Esther answered without thinking, her voice crackling.

He stepped forward, smiling brightly. "Elizabeth, Stephanie—meet Matilda and Esther."

Both women froze—he remembered their names.

Stephanie offered a delicate, rehearsed handshake; Elizabeth merely nodded. A few brittle pleasantries followed—the concert, the weather, the beauty of the hall—all of it perfunctory small talk that evaporated in the charged air between them.

Then he lingered a moment longer, leaning in closely. "I hope everything will be to your liking," he said. "It will be easier than I thought. And don't worry—they're on the house."

Matilda and Esther shared a horrified glance.

With a wink and a smile, he straightened up, turned, and rejoined his companions, arm in arm, toward the far end of the lobby. He said something and the three of them laughed. Other concertgoers began to crowd about him, all offering praise.

Matilda and Esther stood silent, the din of the crowd suddenly distant, like the sea receding before a storm.

A soft chime sounded—the signal for the second half. The two women numbingly made their way to their seats. Esther opened her program. Her eyes caught the bold type face: *Augustus Villano Vidaraski*.

Her mind flickered to the memory of that afternoon, his promising her, *"It might take me a day or two…"* Now he assured her, *"It will be easier than I thought."* Yet what was even more worrisome was his cryptic comment: *"Don't worry—they're on the house."*

What did it mean?

Esther turned the pages of the program. *Mozart's Requiem Mass—his final unfinished masterpiece—is one of the most powerful meditations on death ever composed.*

Mozart gives voice to the full spectrum of human response to death: lament, fear, awe, grief, and trust, ultimately transforming mourning into mercy and despair into hope.

Esther hoped that was true.

The house lights dimmed once more. The conductor raised his baton.

Mozart's *Requiem Mass* began.

The orchestra and chorus surged with beauty and fury—the *Dies Irae* thundering through the rafters, the *Lacrimosa* dissolving into tears.

Esther read the concert notes: *Mozart's Requiem, from the fugal intensity of the Kyrie to the serene majesty of the Domine Jesu, gives voice to every shade of human grief and awe.*

But for her, the words blurred. Even as the choir rose toward its final *Amen,* offering release and eternal light, there was no consolation or peace for her.

When the last voices faded, a reverent silence held the hall before applause erupted—soft at first, then swelling to thunder. The conductor bowed. The soloists bowed. The chorus stood, radiant with the fatigue of a beauty spent.

But Augustus Villano Vidaraski was nowhere to be seen.

THE GRAND DOORS of Covert Symphony Hall opened, spilling Esther and Matilda out into the cool night. The air smelled faintly of rain and exhaust, and the city lights shimmered on the street.

For a moment Esther thought she could breathe again, but she and Matilda said not a word as they walked side by side down the steps.

From behind them came the hum of conversation. They paused at the curb waiting for the streetlight to change.

Esther drew her coat closer. "What did he mean?"

"I don't know," Matilda answered. "I think he's just a tormented artist with a bizarre sense of humor."

Esther harrumphed. Gus Vidar's voice would not subside: *Painless. Cheap. It will be easier than I thought.*

Then Esther's gaze caught on a figure across the street, beneath the golden light of a streetlamp. It was Gus Vidar. Augustus Villano Vidaraski. He stood alone. His tuxedo jacket hung open, shirt untucked, and bow tie loosened. Smoke curled from the cigarette between his fingers, pale against the dark.

He wasn't looking at the women, but up at the limestone façade of the Symphony Hall, studying the building.

There was something about the stillness of him that unsettled her more than the performance itself.

"Do you think he saw us?" Esther whispered.

"I don't know," Matilda muttered. "Maybe."

Then he turned. His eyes caught the light—unmistakable, deliberate. For an instant, they met hers across the empty street. No smile this time, no pretense. Just a long, unreadable look that made Esther's heart pound like a string still vibrating from the last note of his concerto.

He flicked the cigarette to the curb, turned, and vanished into a waiting car that slid out of the shadows to meet him.

Esther and Matilda watched until the taillights disappeared down the wide avenue.

Esther was overcome with emotion. "Matilda, why did you ever have to bring up River and Cain at the ballfield? Their lives are now at risk!"

"Don't be ridiculous," Matilda laughed nervously. "But you're just as guilty, Esther."

Matilda slipped her arm through Esther's. "Come on," she said gently. "Let's get you home."

The two women walked to the parking lot, their footsteps echoing against the pavement. The music and the faint smell of cigarette smoke—followed them. Somewhere in the distance, a crow cawed twice—harsh, guttural.

The women reached the car. Matilda unlocked it quickly and both women slipped inside.

Matilda started the engine and flipped on the headlamps.

She turned to Esther. "It's over. We're safe. Tonight was beautiful. Let's not let him ruin it."

Esther nodded, but she was sure that Gus was still out there—watching and waiting.

MORNING CAME with birdsong and sunlight, but the warmth did nothing to thaw the dread. Esther sat at her kitchen table, staring into her coffee while the television droned on with a Sunday morning show.

Matilda arrived mid-morning with a basket of pastries. "Good grief, you look like you've seen a ghost," she said. "Sit down. Eat something."

Esther obeyed but kept glancing out the kitchen window. "I don't think he's gone," she said.

"Who?"

"You know who," Esther replied, pursing her lips.

"Stop," Matilda said firmly. "You'll drive yourself mad. He's just a creepy guy."

"But what about that broken piano string?" Esther pleaded. "It was an omen."

"It was a broken string," Matilda shook her head. "Nothing more. You're letting your imagination get to you."

"I know," Esther replied, though her voice faltered. Her hand tightened around her coffee cup. She *knew*.

The sound of the television in the background offered a distraction for the women. The morning news team had been chattering about traffic and weather, but now the anchor's voice suddenly changed.

Esther grabbed the remote control and turned up the volume.

Matilda sat and turned her chair toward the screen as the announcer's voice continued with a montage of video from downtown Covert.

"Breaking news this morning concerning a horrific crime—two men were found dead high atop the roof of the Covert Symphony Hall. Police were called to investigate a report of two bodies that were dangling from the roof of the old opera house. Police now describe the deaths as homicides and one official said that the murders appear to be ritualistic. Details are limited pending investigation. This is an active investigation and we will continue to follow this story. We'll be right back after a word from our sponsors."

The television commercial was an advertisement for a funeral business offering a prepackage plan and discount on a cemetery plot or cremation urn.

Esther's breathing was shallow and her head ached. She reached for her coffee mug, taking a sip.

The news report soon returned: "As we've been reporting this morning, two men were found dead early this morning, apparent victims of murder. Their bodies were discovered bound together, dangling from the roof of the Symphony Hall's old opera house. Details are limited, pending investigation, but a few new details have just been shared with the newsroom: the victims are both males in their twenties, they were discovered bound together and strangled with what authorities believe to be piano wire. Authorities have also positively identified the victims but their names will not be released to the public until their families have been notified. Police have no suspects at this time and no apparent motive for the crimes."

Esther's coffee cup slipped from her hand, spilling her coffee over the table and cascading to the tile floor.

"Esther?" Matilda gasped, reaching for her cup.

"Oh, God!" Esther cried. "It's them—our boys, Cain and River."

"No," Matilda said, shaking her head. "You don't know that"

But the denial rang hollow and her eyes betrayed her disbelief.

Matilda grabbed a kitchen towel and cleaned up the mess.

Gus's casual prophecy—*It might take me a day or two, but I'll get it done for you*—had unfolded with virtuosic precision. *It'll be easier than I thought.*

And they're on the house.

The *Opera* House.

Esther pieced the mystery together.

By afternoon, the same grim images kept replaying on the television news: yellow tape flapping in the wind, surrounding Covert Symphony Hall, detectives climbing on the roof looking for evidence, and authorities placing two body bags into a police van. The news crew's camera also focused on a cardboard sign that was found at the murder scene. The sign had been duct-taped to the murder victims and on it was scrawled a message in black marker.

A Requiem for Losers.

It was a grotesque echo of a joke only the two women understood.

By late afternoon, the news still bled through the house, choking the silence. Outside, the sun dipped low, burning gold against the window blinds.

The two women were fretfully silent.

Finally, Esther spoke. "What if he's not done?"

"We can't go to the police," Matilda said quietly. "They'd never believe us. We have nothing—no proof."

"But he's out there," Esther assured her. "Watching. Waiting."

From somewhere nearby—a neighbor's open window, perhaps—came the faint sound of someone playing a piano.

Then the phone rang.

The women stared at each other, afraid to move.

"Don't answer it," Matilda whispered.

Esther's hand trembled. She lifted the receiver, her voice barely a breath. "Hello?"

Silence. Then, a smooth, unhurried low voice—velvet and venom.

"You're doing very well, Esther. I like that."

Her chest tightened. "Who is this?"

"I think you know."

The voice chuckled softly and the line clicked dead.

Before either woman could speak, a faint knock echoed at the door, as if from a thrown rock.

Esther crept to the window. The street was empty, but from the corner of her eye, she saw it: a piece of paper was stuck in her mailbox. She opened the door and stepped out to her mailbox, heart pounding.

She retrieved the paper slowly.

Just then a crow cawed from the telephone wire, then flapped into the dying sun.

She unfolded the paper.

Scrawled in black marker, the words were jagged, uneven—

Poof. Gone.

Cheap.

Below it, smaller—

Hits for Free.

Esther folded the paper, placed it in her hip pocket, and stepped back inside the house.

Her phone rang again.

It was her daughter, Lisa.

Across the room, Matilda's cell phone began to ring.

CONTRIBUTORS

Jonathan S Baker lives and works in Evansville, Indiana where the bouncers are brutal and the Christmas trees are perfect. They're the author of several books of poetry and host of Indiana's longest-running and most prestigious poetry series, Poetry Speaks.

Joshua Britton is the author of two short story collections, *The Perks of Being Alive* and *Tadpoles*, and the novelette, *Heart Decisions*, and also edited *The Notes Will Carry Me Home*, an anthology of music writings. Joshua has had fiction and non-fiction published in *Cobalt Review*, *Tickets to Midnight*, *Tethered by Letters*, *The Bombay Review*, *Frontier Times*, *The Tarantino Chronicles*, and many more. Also an active freelance trombonist, Joshua has released the solo album, *Just Sayin'*, and fronts the ska-jazz project, Josh and the Britt-Tones. www.joshua-britton.com.

Jessica Harman was born in Montreal in 1974. She holds a B.A. in Creative Writing from Concordia University (Montreal). She attended a session over Zoom, during COVID, at The Writers' Workshop at The University of Iowa. Her poems have appeared in "Arion," "Bellevue Literary Review," "Nimrod," and "Spare Change News." She has lectured on poetry (and phenomenology in poetry) at adult education centers in The Greater Boston Area. She taught Creative Writing at "Go-Getters," a mental health wellness rehabilitation center in Salisbury, Maryland. She has several books of poetry published: "Dream Catcher" (2013) and "The Landscape Revolving around Us" (2019), both from Adrich Pres (Kelsay Books). Another poetry collection, "Drifting Tomatoes," was published by Alien Buddha Press in 2024. Her collection of short stories, "In Praise of One of Rebecca's Strongest Traits," was published by Wilderness House Press in 2020. She has several books of fiction published by Alien Buddha Press, including "A Cup of Truth at The Hard Knock Café" (2021), "Indigestion" (2022), and "Bite the Wax Tadpole" (2024), as well as numerous self-published books on Amazon. She lives in Maryland.

Jay Heltzer is a #5amWritersClub devotee and writes speculative fiction and microfiction. His works have been seen in Paragraph Planet, Five Minutes, and The Prompt Magazine. Jay plays bass trombone around Washington, D.C., but that's a different story, which can be read in his monthly Substack called "Low Notes" where he combines his experience as a musician and shares tales from his ongoing writing journey. Jay can be found on X and Bluesky at @JayHeltzer.

John William McMullen is a writer, philosopher, and theologian, and a student of literature and the arts. His musical interests vary from Gregorian chant and classical to bluegrass and rock. He is the author of assorted short stories, the novel *Poor Souls;* the historical narratives of *The Miracle of Stalag 8A - Beauty Beyond the Horror: Olivier Messiaen and the Quartet for the End of Time;* and *The Last Blackrobe of Indiana and the Potawatomi Trail of Death.* He is currently working on a play and has co-written a screenplay for a historical mini-series. McMullen lives in Evansville, Indiana, with his wife, Mary Grace.

Carina Wahlstrom lives in Southern Indiana. Her stories have been published in *Story Quilt*, *50-Word Stories*, *Night Owl Narrative*, and *The Notes Will Carry Me Home.* The Newport Phantomfighters were inspired by her time as a volunteer firefighter, and the organ in Trinity Church is still played regularly. While the facts surrounding the organ are true, ghosts have yet to be sighted.

Daniel W. Wright is a poet, editor, and fiction writer. Wright is the author of poetry chapbook Gods of a Former World (Crying Heart Press, 2025), the full-length poetry collection The Unheard Music (Kung Fu Treachery, 2025), and the novel Call Center (Back of the Class, 2024). He is also the author of four other full-length collections of poetry, five poetry chapbooks, a novella, a short story collection, and co-author of four poetry splits. His work has appeared in numerous print and online journals including Chiron Review, Book of Matches, and Gasconade Review. Wright currently resides in St. Louis, MO where you can usually find him in a bar or a bookstore.